"DEATH HAS OPENED HIS JAWS. WOULD YOU WALK INTO THEM?"

Pryderi tried to speak patiently. "You do not understand. You do not come of the blood of the Lords of Dyved. I do, and I accept the destiny that is laid on me."

Manawyddan's hand dropped; he understood. Sadly the son of Llyr watched that straight young figure stride down the hill and into the white-rimmed mouth of the Mound of Testing. Night came before he abandoned his vigil and returned to Arberth.

When Rhiannon saw that he was alone, her eyes became spears piercing him. "Where is he that was with you? Man without honor, without courage!"

As flame darts over dry leaves, she darted past him, and was gone.

By *Evangeline Walton:*

The Books of the Welsh Mabinogion

Published by Ballantine Books

The Song of Rhiannon

by

Evangeline Walton

~L ~L ~L

The Third Branch of the Mabinogion

A Del Rey Book

BALLANTINE BOOKS • NEW YORK

TO MY MOTHER,
Who had a bright and gallant spirit.

CONTENTS

On Evangeline Walton—and Magic

(from "The Saturday Review" by Patrick Merla)

"... The essential element of any true work of fantasy is magic—a force that affects the lives and actions of all the creatures that inhabit the fantasist's world. This magic may be innate or manifest; it may be used by the characters who live with it, or come from 'gods' of the author's contrivance. Always it is a *supernatural* force whose use, *mis*use, or *dis*use irrevocably changes the lives of those it touches.

. . . Now, magic is like religion and politics: few people agree about it. . . . I believe in magic. Not as mystic mumbo jumbo, but as a way of life. . . . Having long been a student of mysticism (Oriental and Occidental), I have observed that a magical substructure underlies the best fantasies. A book's setting may be Khendiol (*Red Moon and Black Mountain*), King Arthur's England (*The Once and Future King*), or ancient Wales (*The Mabinogion*), but its magic is Real Magic, an archetypal life-giving quality, consistent with magic as it has always been. (In a way this 'cosmic uniformity' is similar to the astonishing similarity of the poetry of Kabir, Rumi, and St. John of the Cross—three mystics from different eras and cultures, all of whom wrote about their religious experiences in almost identical terms.)

There are as many ways of enjoying fantasy books as

there are volumes. A comparison of works derived in some way from *The Mabinogion* (The Druidic books of legends of the Welsh people)—both from a literary standpoint and as magical expositions—may give readers an idea of the nature of successful fantasy.

J. R. R. Tolkien and Joy Chant have both made use of magical archetypes found in *The Mabinogion* to enrich their own books; Evangeline Walton's books, on the other hand, are actual retellings of these diverse legends in novel form. Each of these works deals with the struggle between the forces of Good and Evil. Each of them presents some form of quest. Three of them deal with the nature of love.

. . . Not even Tolkien can create names more magical than those found in *The Mabinogion* itself. (Of course, the Druids were wielders of Real Magic.) In one sense, therefore, Evangeline Walton had some of her work already done for her before she began to write her tetralogy based on the four 'branches' of *The Mabinogion*. These books, together with C. S. Lewis's *Out of the Silent Planet, Perelandra,* and *That Hideous Strength* and T. H. White's *The Once and Future King,* are not only the best fantasies of the twentieth century. They are also great works of fiction.

. . . The wonders of Walton's books are manifold. . . . I suspect that Evangeline Walton knows something about magic from personal experience. Her books are so thoroughly steeped in mysticism that mere anthropological knowledge of Druidical lore is insufficient to explain their authority. Only C. S. Lewis has matched Walton's subtle depiction of the forces of Good and Evil.

. . . Walton succeeds in creating an imaginary world that we believe *actually existed* in this world's history. She is able to do what few writers of worth would dare attempt: to predict a future we have already witnessed —this century's wars—and to make that prediction credible in the context of the past she presents.

In Walton's realm of Gwynedd magic does not disappear when materialism enters the scene—as it does in Tolkien's book and in most of the works drawn from

The Mabinogion. It merely becomes invisible to men who would not wish to see it if they could. . . ."

The Song of Rhiannon

The Last of the Children of Llyr

They turned their faces westward, toward the ancient path of the dead, those seven who were seeking a new life. Those seven who alone had come back from Ireland and from that great war that had stripped two islands of warriors; that war in which not only their comrades but the life and the ways of life they knew had died.

It was too late that day for them to get far on their way to Dyved, so they made camp outside Llwndrys, within sight of the White Mount, where they had buried the Head of Bran their King, he who once had been called the Blessed. They saw the moon rise, tipping with silver the trees and thatched roofs of that city of kings. And then sleep came to weight down their eyelids, and six of the seven slept. Only Manawyddan son of Llyr still sat wakeful, and thought of all that had been, and no longer was.

He looked toward the thatched roof of the King's Hall, and remembered how his parents had taken him and Bran there as little children, to visit great Beli, their uncle: and how long Bran had dreamed that Caradoc his son might sit there, Lord of that hall where no king's son ever before had been enthroned. For the Old Tribes counted descent through the mother, and a king's sister's son always had followed him as Bran had followed Beli.

But now Caradoc was under the earth with Bran, and Caswallon, son of Beli, sat in that hall, safe in the place that he had won by magic and by murder. Bran's dream had been fulfilled, though not in the way that he had dreamed it. A king's son now sat in the seat of his father, and the days and the ways of the Old Tribes were done.

Manawyddan sat there and saw nothingness. He heard it and felt it, he tasted it and breathed it.

Had he been younger, he might have sought vengeance; have kindled and fed its fires, and found in them a refuge. An aim for the aimless, warmth in that great cold.

I could do it, I am still a strong man. But if I did it, more men would die; surely some of these six faithful comrades beside me. Young Pryderi himself might die, he for whom life can still hold much. I could do the deed alone, but how? Creep upon my foe from behind, like a wolf? As he crept upon the chiefs that Bran left to guard Caradoc? Make myself over to fit his pattern? No. Better to die cleanly, in a ditch, like any other wandering beggar.

For what are you but a beggar, Manawyddan, son of Llyr, who have nowhere to go? For whom all roads lead nowhere.

That was true. He had nothing left to do, no place to go, now that Bran's last order had been fulfilled, and the Head laid in Its chosen resting-place.

If only you were alive, Branwen, little sister! If

only your child had lived, or Caradoc. But Bran's dream was the torch; it lit the fire that brought red ruin upon all of us . . .

All the years of his manhood he had served Bran and the Island of the Mighty: and though he had done his own thinking and sometimes Bran's, he never had done anything for himself, for his own gain. He felt afraid now, stripped and helpless and afraid, as he never could have felt had there been anyone left for him to work and fight for. Nobody is so dependent upon others as the unselfish man; their need is his fuel and his balance, so that he needs them and that need is itself perhaps a queer kind of selfishness. When Manawyddan had had dependents, he had had infinite resource. But now he had neither, and nothing.

He sat through that night and saw dawn come, like a faded, gray-haired woman painting her withered cheeks. He saw the sun raise her bright head in the east, begin her steady and inexorable march, that march which called all other men to work and life.

He rose; he cried out as a man upon the dizzy edge of a precipice might cry, "O Almighty Mothers! Oh, my sorrow! There is none but me that does not know where he shall lay his head this night!"

"Lord—" The voice was Pryderi's. That youngest and dearest of the seven had awakened. He stumbled to his feet, still awkward with sleep, and came forward. And Manawyddan was silent, ashamed.

"Lord—" The young King of Dyved's hand was on his arm.

"It is not a bed or a roof I mean, lad. Those are little things—no beggar that wanders the Island of the Mighty but can have them, for knocking upon any decent farmer's door. It is a place I mean, something that belongs to me and I to it. Wherever I go, I will be a stranger. It is an exile I am now, upon all the earth, with Bran and Branwen under sod, and all my kindred dead."

Pryderi was silent, trying to think. In that weakness of the strong man, of the oak without ivy, was something that it seemed indecent to look upon, such horror as later men might feel in seeing a tortured man's body naked in its helplessness.

"Lord, your cousin is king over the Island of the Mighty. You and he are of one blood, and in your youth you were friends. He sits in your place —I know that—but you never have laid claim to land or possessions. Always you have been known as the Third Landless Prince. And Caswallon needs peace as this land needs it—he would be glad to have you beside him to help him make it. As you helped Bran."

"He might indeed." Manawyddan laughed shortly. "The last of the sons of my mother his house dog, and all tongues silenced! But though this man is my cousin, I could not bear to see him in the seat of my brother, the Blessed. Never could I know happiness in one house with Caswallon!"

What more he might have said he did not say; the boy's intended kindness bound him. So this was what all men would think, even his faithful six. That because he, now the rightful High King, did not seek his heritage, he was willing to be Caswallon's tamed hound. A new height of loneliness opened before him, a new depth of pain.

Pryderi was silent again, biting his lip and thinking. Then of a sudden his eyes brightened. He straightened his shoulders like one casting off a load. His white teeth gleamed in an eager, beguiling smile. "Lord, would you be willing to listen to any more advice?"

"I stand in need of advice," Manawyddan answered wearily. He felt no interest, he spoke from courtesy only; but Pryderi seized upon that permission as joyously as a dog seizes upon a bone.

"Lord, seven cantrevs came to me from Pwyll my father; in them Rhiannon my mother dwells. With my wife Kigva I live in the Seven Cantrevs of Seissyllwch, and if you were my mother's man you two could enjoy my father's lands together. None are fairer or richer—it would make my heart glad for you to have them."

For a breath's space Manawyddan was silent; then he said, "I thank you for great friendship, Prince. Your mother might not; she is well able to choose her own man if she wanted one."

"I would show you the best friendship in the world if you would let me," Pryderi coaxed. "The Lady my mother would say what I say—ever since I was little I have heard her praise you as the noblest of men. Never has she forgotten that one visit of yours to Dyved, long ago. And she is lonely now, with my father dead and me a married man."

Manawyddan opened his mouth to say no, but

as he did so, a golden bird flew overhead. A golden feather fell at his feet. He stooped to pick it up; in his hand the thing shone like light, and as he looked at it, he heard his own voice say, to his own wonder, "I will go with you, lad. To Rhiannon."

2

They Come to the Shepherd's Hut

So they set out for Dyved by the western sea, and one by one their comrades left them; went back to their own homes to tell there such tales as old soldiers have always told. Surely no old soldiers ever can have told bigger ones, though that is saying much. For no other men on earth yet have fought against foes who held the Cauldron of Rebirth, that even when outraged and held captive in this gross world of ours, still had power to raise the dead. To send their unsouled bodies back, possessed by demons of the Underworld, to fight against living men.

Gluneu was the first to go. He left them that second night; and when the six lay down to sleep, Manawyddan groped for that shining feather and could not find it. He smiled wryly, without surprise. *Well, so I only dreamed. The Birds of Rhiannon are with her in Arberth, they that alone came with her from her own world. And I am not the man for whom she left it.*

For Pwyll she had given up everlasting youth; for him she, the daughter of a King in Faery, had put on mortal flesh and its pain. To get Pwyll and to keep him, she had borne many trials; and at

7

last the uttermost had been required of her: to sit alone, through the withering years.

I will visit her, then go. So far my promise binds me. Yet deep within the son of Llyr something still stirred, as nothing had stirred since Bran had got his poisoned wound and had said, "Cut off my head." Memory that, for a space, could drive back even that black memory. *You cannot have forgotten, Queen, any more than I have forgotten. I did you a great service, yet because of that very service you may never wish to look upon my face again.*

She would not show that; she was a true Queen. They would meet and part graciously; one more parting should not matter much, in this time of many partings.

On the third day Ynawc left them. Grudyen went next, and then Heilyn. Taliesin was the last to go, he the sweet singer, the wonder of western bards until the world's end. Pryderi tried hard to get him to go on to Dyved.

"You can get the best hospitality in the world there," he urged. "You can sing with my mother's Birds, that some say can sing even sweeter than you, and you can talk wisdom with my kinsman, the old druid Pendaran Dyved."

But Taliesin shook his head.

"I have been with you long enough," he said, "and the deeds we shall do together are done. I would they were not, for you are both good company. But I must go where new deeds are shaping, for that is ever the law of Taliesin. You ride south into Dyved that men unborn shall call the Land of

Illusion and Glamour, and I ride north, into the fierce sunlight of the future."

Manawyddan looked at him straightly. "You mean that we are the past? Well, so it may be."

Pryderi put his hands to his hips and hitched his sword around a little.

"I do not feel past at all," said he. "I am still doing things, and I intend to do more."

But Taliesin and Manawyddan did not heed him; they were looking deep into each other's eyes. The twilight was soft around them; under the trees dusk was settling, shadows that soon would ripen into darkness were already stretching forth long black arms. Only pink clouds still bloomed like flowers in the western sky. And for a breath's space the gay young King of Dyved felt as though he were touched by the fingertip of a great silence, of a finality that was also peace. Then the poet turned to him.

"I go now, to Gwynedd," said Taliesin. "I was there at the court of Don, before the birth of Gwydion. And now I would watch him grow."

"Gwydion?" said Pryderi, pleased to understand something at last. "Is he not the little boy who will be Mâth's heir?"

In the dim light Taliesin looked at him long and sadly. "He is a little boy, but that is not all he is. Or all he has been. He has borne many names. But now he is called the son of Don, the sister of Mâth the Ancient, and in time to come you will think that you know that name too well. And later all the world will know him, for there is a universal forge, and our world is metal upon it, and he is the smith who will hammer our part of the world into a new shape. What bloody fools like Caswallon do may be undone, but not the work of wise men who work through the mind."

"He has a great destiny on him," said Pryderi, impressed. "Maybe one that the rest of us could do without. Why should I think that I know him too well?"

Taliesin did not answer and Manawyddan rubbed his chin. "I remember now; a thing that Mâth once said. He knows already that this child has come to undo his work and do his own."

"He knows and accepts," said Taliesin. "What can be hidden from Mâth the Ancient? In the Eastern World there is a God, men say, who loathed change and its evils as Mâth does, and wished to keep His people at peace and in the Golden Age. So He forbade them to eat of the fruit of the Tree of Knowledge, and was disobeyed. But Mâth is a wiser God than that; He will not forbid his people to do what, soon or late, they are bound to do, and so lay upon them the sin of disobedience."

"That is because Math still wears a human body," said Manawyddan, "and can speak for Himself, instead of through the mouths of priests who cannot fully understand His Word."

Pryderi stared. "Mâth is a man. A man of Illusion and Glamour, but human. He eats and sleeps and does all the things the rest of us do. When his time comes he will die."

"All Gods die," said Taliesin. "By dying as a man a God can sometimes show most clearly that He is a God. But now the time comes for Mâth to withdraw from earth and cease to be worshipped for awhile, for now men want fiercer Gods."

"As it may be that that Eastern God is," said Manawyddan, "for He is a Father, while we bow to the Mothers. But I do not believe those who call Him jealous. The jealousy must be on His priests. No God would ever be such a fool as to wish to keep His people forever in ignorance, for the ignorant can never choose between good and evil and so master neither."

"All this goes over my head," said Pryderi, and scratched it. "But anyhow it will take this Gwydion of yours, who sounds like an upsetting sort of person, some time to grow up and begin making trouble."

So Taliesin the Much-Remembering left them, he who has had many births and will have many more. Who may be somewhere among us even now, though nobody knows where. At least nobody who will tell . . .

Pryderi made one more attempt to keep him.

"Indeed," he urged with his loveliest grin, "if you want to be around when somebody is rearing a son, it is with us you should stay. Kigva and I would have had a boy before now, if I had not had to go to war, and it is no time we will be losing now. Indeed, it may be that we already have one," he mused hopefully. "That was a good night, our last before I left Dyved. Triplets might have come of it."

But again Taliesin only shook his head and smiled . . .

So the Seven became Two and went on alone toward Dyved. And the Preseli Mountains guided them westward, those rugged, sky-piercing walls whose tops they had been able to see from Ireland in the bad days. To Pryderi then their sunlit craggy heights had seemed like the sight of a face from home, the home that he was not quite sure that he would ever see again.

Now no sea held him from them, only wild stretches of wood and moor that grew ever narrower beneath his eager feet. And Manawyddan, who would have been glad of a slower pace, knew what was in his heart, panted and kept pace with him.

Night found them in a fold of those windy hills, and there they came upon a shepherd's hut. He made them welcome, but he was old and his eyes were dim, so he did not recognize Pryderi. And Manawyddan said, "Let him think you a stranger; so he may speak more freely than before his Lord. You have been long away from Dyved; much may have happened."

The truth was that ever since he entered those wild lands his druid sight had told him that eyes watched them; hungry, brooding eyes. Maybe the eyes of Caswallon's druids far away, maybe those of druids serving some nearby foe who sought to ambush Pryderi on his way home.

To the shepherd he said, "I am a harper back from the war, and this is Guri, my son."

The shepherd's wife gave them supper, and watched them eat. Then the old woman said, "What war is this you speak of? I did not know that this Island had men enough left, or that those few who still live had heart enough in them to be fighting again. But that is the way of you men. Never resting, always after each other's blood."

"We fought in Ireland," said Manawyddan, "Ireland, where the young men of the Island of the Mighty died. And we do not want to see more death."

She stared. "No man came alive out of that great fighting, surely. Not one has come back to our hills; or to the plains below."

"There are always a few left to come back," said Manawyddan. "Even though they come slowly. We are only the first you have heard of."

The old shepherd leaned forward eagerly. "If you were there—there where the battle roared and later the wolves and the eagles fed on the flesh of our sons—you may know what befell our young Lord. He died there: Pryderi, the son of Pwyll."

"Maybe not," said Pryderi. "Maybe he will come back."

The old man shook his head. "He would have come back before now had he lived. To his people and his mother and his young wife."

"I have come back," said Pryderi. "Do you think my strength and my luck were greater than his?"

"The Mothers alone know what luck is." The old woman peered harder at him through the smoke. "You are like him. He was called Guri too; Guri of the Golden Hair was the name that was on him as a babe, and he grew up to be tall and golden—like you. But he did not come back."

"Is there trouble on Dyved?" asked Manawyddan. "Lordless folk often fare ill."

The shepherd shook his head again. "Not yet. But it is coming. The two Queens still reign in peace, with old Pendaran Dyved to counsel them, Pwyll's wise High Druid. But Caswallon sends gifts to our chief men, and the young men grow restless and mutter, 'We should have a King again.' "

"Then neither Queen has taken a new husband?" Manawyddan asked.

"No. But as soon as Pendaran Dyved is mounded, both will be bedded. Maybe by several husbands apiece before one man proves himself master and can settle down to grind underfoot and plunder those of us who are left."

"And Caswallon would let such things be?" Pryderi's hands clenched. "Never could they have happened under Bran!"

The old man laughed bitterly. "But the Blessing went from Bran the Blessed. He went away and left his son to rule us, contrary to the ancient Law. And now he and all his house are dead, and Caswallon says that he was always the rightful King. And maybe he is right, for clearly the Gods are with him. The Mothers grow weak, the Father grows strong."

Manawyddan was silent. He thought, *This is what all folk must be saying. Victory proves a man the Gods' chosen, even if he be a murderer. And once all men loved and praised you, Bran my brother!*

Yet at the last Bran had broken the peace he had upheld; had undone his own work, and brought misery and death upon his people. That was true, and that truth was the hardest of all things to bear.

Pryderi said stubbornly, "It is the business of a

High King to maintain order and justice. Not to let Under Kings butcher each other and their folk."

Now the old woman laughed, a harsh, shrill cackle. "He needs friends—Caswallon, the Father's choice. The seven chiefs he slew so as to oust Caradoc the son of Bran have left kinsmen and friends. Their hands reach out fast enough to take Caswallon's gifts, but their hearts do not love him. And if his luck goes bad, if crops fail or invaders come, many will cry, 'It is the curse of blood—the blood he shed!' So long as Under Kings call him High King, Caswallon will let them do as they please."

"Or play one of them against another to gain time," said Manawyddan. "Also to see their strength weaken while his grows."

"And Dyved is still a rich and prosperous land!" Pryderi's laugh was like the sound of ripping silk. "He would like well to see it weak and torn—as we left Ireland weak and torn!"

"Maybe so." The old man sighed. "Some say he backs one of our Lords, some that he backs another. But all these greedy lordlings are only waiting for the breath to be out of Pendaran Dyved's body. Fear of the old druid's curse still holds all men back, but he is failing. His end nears."

"I should think that Rhiannon herself could do a bit of cursing," said Pryderi. "She is no mortal-born Queen."

"Oh, she has her magics!" The old woman cackled again. "I would like well to have a tiny part of that magic! But it never was of a kind to keep men off her, and even in her youth she had no power to curse those lying women who swore that she had killed her own babe. None need fear her!"

"To have sent sickness or death on those women could not have cleared her," said Manawyddan. "Only have made folk fear and hate her more. I have heard that tale."

"You have? It is told in many ways. But I know the rights of it." And she launched into the telling, eager as a starving man sitting down to meat; all the troubles that were and would be forgotten in the wonders and now unterrifying terrors of the past.

Manawyddan thought wearily, *Here in this lonely place a chance to talk means much to her. And perhaps she is wiser than she seems. To forget what one cannot strive against—to enjoy what one still has—there are worse ways to dream away one's days. The question is: if one searched hard enough, might one still find a way to do, instead of to dream?*

He knew the tale she was telling better than she did. He let flow from his mind into hers such hidden parts of it as he thought it safe for her to know.

"Here on Preseli it all began." Her voice had risen to a chant. "Here the chief men of Dyved gathered to meet Pwyll their Lord. In the Holy Place they awaited him, within that double ring of bluestones where folk have met in council since first men walked in Dyved. Old, old are those rings, and in the dark night their tall Stones rise and dance together. For they are the Eldest Folk, the firstborn of Earth the Mother. Each has a

name that may not be spoken, and each has power
to heal or blast. And no man dare go back upon
the word he has spoken before them; else he
would wither and die."

"I know of that place," said Manawyddan.
"Great is the power of the outer ring, but that of
the inner is yet greater. For its twelve Stones are
said to be the first Twelve Gods born of Earth,
archetype of all the mighty mysterious Twelves
that are to come. In their sides is not only the
color of the sea that once covered all things, but
the ashes of those fires from which Earth the
Mother shaped Herself, that mighty travail from
which the mountains and the valleys sprang.*

The old woman stared at him, her jaw drop-
ping. "You know too much. You can be no man of
the New Tribes!"

"Good men spring from all tribes, woman.
Were not your Pwyll and his Pryderi born of the
New?"

The shepherd said sadly, "Yes. They have been
gentle conquerors, the House of Pwyll. But those
who come after them will be hard on the little
man; on us shepherds and tillers of the soil. They
will make all who spring from the Old Tribes
little."

"Not forever," said Manawyddan. "In the end
Old Tribes and New will become one folk."

"Maybe. But it will take yet longer—long and
long—for the rich to become brothers to the poor."

---

*Only from Preseli could the "bluestone circles" of Stone-
henge have been brought. though their moving would have
been a herculean, almost incredible task for any ancient
people.

"The House of Pwyll may not be ended," Pryderi cut in, his jaw set.

"Those men who met Pwyll in the Holy Place wanted to keep it from ending." The old woman went on with her tale again, firmly. "Pwyll came, and he said, 'Men, why have you sent for me?' And they said, 'Lord, we are sorrowful to see a man we love so much, our chief and our foster-brother, without an heir. You are not so young as some of us, and your wife is childless. Take another, and get sons. You cannot stay with us always, and though you may wish to keep the woman you have, we will not suffer it.' They did not say, 'That woman out of Faery is mortal now, and can be killed. Her own people will not avenge her, they whose wrath must have put barrenness on her. And if you do, we will bear it for love of you.'

"They did not say that, because it would not have been good manners, but Pwyll knew what they meant. He knew, too, his duty to his people. He said, 'The woman and I have slept together only three winters, and there is still time for her belly to swell. Give me a year and a day, and if it has not, I will do according to your will.' And they agreed.

"On May Day that pact was made, and on the next May Eve—in the very nick of time, just one night before her time was up—Queen Rhiannon bore a son. By what arts she got him the Mothers alone know, but get him she did. And she and her Lord were triumphant as warriors who ride home from battle, laden with spoil. Pwyll and his men made merry in the great hall, and in her great bed the Queen slept, and her babe slept beside her.

Six of the noblest ladies of Dyved watched over them, so all seemed safe. Even though May Eve is one of the Holy Nights when the doors between the worlds open—when those who have put off our flesh or never worn it can come from their terrible unearthly places against us mortals.

"They cannot have been happy, those six fine ladies—each of them had a daughter or a sister that she said would have brought Pwyll four fine boys in those four winters instead of only one. A bitter pill it must have been, too, to know that now, because of her one son, this stranger woman would queen it over them forever. But they dared not say so; they had to pretend to be proud and happy. For no higher trust could have been given to any women in Dyved. They knew that they must guard that mother and son as each would her own two eyes. Yet by midnight every last one of them was fast asleep."

Here her husband managed to put a word in. "You can't blame them for that, old woman. That sleep must have been sent upon them, by Those the wise do not name."

She went on as if he had not spoken. "And toward daybreak, when they woke, all six of them, with a great start—the boy was gone. He was not there; he was not anywhere; it was as if there never had been a boy at all. Then great fear took them, who had slept when they should have kept watch, who, as many would bear witness, had whispered against their Queen, the stranger . . . "

Behind his hand Pryderi yawned and whispered to Manawyddan, "I never thought that I should ever have to listen to this yarn again." Then his mouth grew grim. "If I had been my father, I would have drowned all those miserable hags like rats."

"And they the wives and sisters of his chief men? You know better than that, boy."

"So my mother says. That if he had, there would not yet have been peace in Dyved. But I still say . . . "

"Hush, lad! Our hostess will hear you!"

Indeed, the woman had stopped talking and was looking at them indignantly, but such a great silence promptly settled upon them that they looked as if it had been there forever, and she went on.

"The Queen still slept, so they killed a staghound bitch's newborn pup and smeared her face and hands with the blood, then laid the bones beside her. Then they rose up and scratched their own faces and blacked each others' eyes and screamed aloud, so that the whole court came running in. And they pointed to the bloodied face of the sleeping Queen and cried out upon her. 'Would to the Mothers that you had come when we called in the night! For this madwoman rose up and such demon's strength was on her that all of us together could not hold her. Before our eyes she tore her own son limb from limb and ate him raw!'

"So was joy turned to sorrow, and triumph to woe. Like fire the tale spread through the land, and his nobles came again to Pwyll. 'Put away this evil woman, Lord, this murderess who has devoured her own flesh and yours.' But Pwyll answered, 'You have no right to ask that. I agreed to put her away if she was barren, but now she has given birth. Keep your bargain, as I have kept mine.' But still they raged, and at last, lest she be butchered or burned alive behind his back, he had to say, 'Let the druids judge her.'

"And Rhiannon begged those women, 'By the sun and by the moon, who see all, by the Mothers in Whose shape we are all fashioned, charge me not falsely! If you lie because fear is on you, I will defend you.'

"But they answered, 'Truly, Lady, not for anyone in the wide world would we risk bringing evil upon ourselves.'

"'Is not my woe great enough?' said Rhiannon. 'The sorrow of a mother that has lost her child? What evil will come upon you for telling the truth?'

"But whatever she said, she got only one answer from those women.

"So in the end the druids came and heard all, and this is the doom they spoke: 'Lady, for seven years you shall sit every day upon the horse block before your Lord's house here in Arberth. And to every one that comes to his door you shall tell the tale of your bloody deed, and then bow down upon all fours—even as a beast would go, she that knows no better than to eat her own young—and bear that guest on your back into the hall.'

"Such was the judgment of the druids, and as they ordered, so it was done. But few would ride upon her back, for we folk of Dyved have hearts in our breasts."

3

The Man Who Fought the Monster

Then, because her own throat was parched, the old woman rose and fetched mead for them all. When Manawyddan praised its rare goodness, she smiled and said, "I have a little friend that helps me."

"A bogey, I suppose. More magic," said Pryderi. "Surely my father and all his men must have been magicked, not to know a pup's bones from mine. Those misbegotten hags would have done better to say that the bitch swallowed me whole, and that my mother had made a breakfast of raw pup to get even."

"Lad, do you want her to hear you?"

But because Pryderi's young jaw was set and his eyes smoldered the old woman poured him the fullest cup of the sweet yellow mead. Flattered because her tale had so moved him, she sat down by the fire and began again.

"Teyrnon of the Thunder-Flood was Lord of Gwent then, and there was no better man in the world. And he had a mare, and in all the land no horse or mare was more beautiful. But though every May Eve, in the dark of night, she foaled, in the morning there never was any foal beside her. What became of her colts no man ever knew. And one night Teyrnon talked with his wife. 'Woman,' he said, 'it is great fools we are, to let our mare foal every year and never get a single one of her colts.'

" 'What can we do about it' said she.

" 'Tomorrow night is May Eve,' he said. 'And may I never look upon sun or moon again if I do not find what the Thing is that comes and carries away the colts!'

"She was frightened and tried to stop him, but he would not listen. He had the mare led into an empty hut, the last and least of the small houses grouped round his great house. On one side of it was the open moor, and on the other a door, the only opening. He had his men build up a bright fire, then bade them leave and shut the door behind them, for a bitter wind was blowing in from the moor. He sat himself down, fully armed, against the wall farthest from that door. There he could watch unseen, for thick shadows covered him. He waited there until the gray twilight ceased to try to force its fingers through the cracks round the door, and there was no light left at all but the red glow of the fire. The wind howled and the mare stood by the fire and shivered. Now and then she lifted her head and neighed pitifully, and it seemed to Teyrnon that her dark eyes looked in fear at the door. But he kept still and did not go to her, though he was a man whose nature it was to go to the help of all beasts in pain.

"Night had scarce fallen when she foaled—a big, beautiful he-colt. It stood up on wobbling legs, weak and wet and dazed, and the mother washed it. The feel of her tongue comforted it and it pressed closer and found her teats and sucked; it was happy again then, as it had been inside the warm dark nest of her body. So they comforted each other after the squeezing, rending pangs of birth; and so the foal, like all young, discovered this huge world and himself, and her who was the first sharer of its great and terrible loneliness.

"Teyrnon could not stand it any longer. He went to them and praised the mare and felt over the foal with his hands, proud of its size and of the strength with which it sucked.

"But even as he knelt beside them, a great crash came and the door fell in. Through the black opening a huge arm darted, thick as a tree and blacker than the night, and at the end of it a great, gleaming claw that grasped the colt's mane. Teyrnon sprang up and hacked at it with his sword, and when the mare saw that this time she had help, she too sprang upon the Arm, biting and kicking. Teyrnon needed her; he had been Pwyll, Prince of Dyved's man, and had fought beside him in many battles, yet never had he met a foe like this. His sword seemed to be hewing wood, and all three of them—man, mare, and colt—were being steadily, if slowly dragged through the doorway. Power to hinder that unearthly Power they had, but stop it they could not. And then all at once Teyrnon's blade worked through mighty muscle and sinew to the bone itself. Harder than rock that bone seemed, and at first Teyrnon thought that all was over, but he shut his eyes and held his breath and smote with all his strength. And then there rose up a shriek like no other shriek ever heard in this world; it seemed to fill all the space beneath the sky and to shake Earth herself. Teyrnon reeled back, his eardrums all but splitting, and when his head cleared he saw that the Arm, all its terrible black length, up to where the elbow should have been, lay there severed. Around it boiled a great pool of blood, from which rose a stench that all but choked him.

"On one side of the door the wall had been ripped like cloth and the roof sagged. He set his shoulder against that wreckage and broke through it, for that stinking, boiling blood blocked the doorway. He led out the mare and her foal, though she screamed as only a horse can scream and rolled her eyes, for the night was still filled with unearthly wailing. They stood there, all three of them, and gulped in deep breaths of the clean night air, and gradually the wailing dimmed, as that monstrous, wounded Thing, fleeing, sank back into the depths of the Underworld, into that unspeakable, unthinkable darkness from which it had come. And then through that wailing they heard another wail; a small sharp cry out there in the dark night.

" 'What is that?' cried Teyrnon, and he ran forward.

"Near the doorway he found it, where it had fallen, just clear of the blood that still boiled from that monstrous, bleeding Arm. A baby, wrapped in a mantle of shining stuff, and yelling as if it would split its small fat throat.

"Teyrnon picked it up and unwrapped it and looked it over as he had the colt, and then he looked toward the colt itself and grinned.

" 'You are a pair, the two of you,' he said. 'Both newborn and both stallions.'

"He saw that the foal had found its mother's teat again, need rising above the memory of terror, and how the mother was quieting, standing still to assuage that need, though her whole body still trembled. His face sobered and he looked down again at the screeching baby.

" 'Well, that one of you who is four-legged seems to be the luckier now. We will take you inside, Master Two-legs, and see what we can do about that. I cannot see why people have not come running out to see what is the matter.'

"He went back into his great hall and found all there, men, women, and children, fast asleep. As fast asleep as the six ladies who, that same night, were watching beside Rhiannon's bed. But of them, of course, he knew nothing. He went on and came to his own sleeping chamber, and there he found his wife, as sound asleep as any of the others. He shook her and when her eyes opened and she stared at him, he grinned again.

" 'Is this the woman that was not going to close either eye all night for fear of what might be happening to me?'

"She might have looked sheepish then, but at that instant the baby, who had stopped for lack of wind, got its breath back and began to cry again. That was a sound she must often have longed for, she who was a childless wife, even as Rhiannon had been. But now it made her give a great start.

" 'Lord, what is that?'

"Teyrnon, still grinning, held the baby out to her.

" 'Woman, here is a boy for you, if you will have him you never gave birth to.'

" 'Who did give birth to him?' she said. And she sat up very straight, and looked at Teyrnon very hard.

" 'This is what happened,' and Teyrnon told her all. She marveled much at that hearing, and she gave many little squeaks, both for terror at his danger, and of praise for his valor, but never did her eyes leave the child. And when she had warmed milk for it and changed its swaddling clothes, that by then were very wet indeed, and it slept at last, satisfied, she held up the shining mantle and looked at it with a careful, appraising eye.

" 'This is good stuff; rare stuff. She that owned this mantle was rich enough to deck herself and her son in all the treasures of the Eastern world.' And she looked at Teyrnon and thought with relief that he did not know any such woman, and that if he ever had, it had been too long ago for her to have borne him this son tonight.

" 'The boy is of gentle blood,' she said.

" 'He is a fine boy anyhow,' said Teyrnon. 'Strong for his age.'

" 'His age!' She snorted. 'He has no age—he who was born this very night.' Her eyes widened suddenly. 'Lord, let us have a game; a merry game with my women. We will call them in and say that I have been pregnant these many moons, but dared say nothing lest it come to nothing, I to whom the Mothers have not been kind.'

"So it was done, though I who am a woman do not think that the women of Teyrnon's household

can have been fooled. Likely Teyrnon's wife
wanted to see all of them as soon as she could to
make sure that none of them showed signs of child-
birth, shining cloak or no shining cloak—and likely
they thought it wise not to contradict their mis-
tress. Anyhow, most of Gwent—certainly all the
men in it—believed the child to be Teyrnon's own
son by his lady. They named the boy Guri, and
because what hair was on his head was pure gold,
they called him Guri of the Golden Hair. And by
the next May Eve he was walking briskly and was
as big as the biggest child three years old."

"This woman thinks well of me," whispered
Pryderi to Manawyddan. "When I heard that tale
at home I was only as big and fine as the biggest,
finest boy of one year could be."

"That seems more likely," Manawyddan whispered back, "but be still."

"And by the second year," the old woman went
on, "he was as big and fine as the biggest, finest
child six years old."

Here Pryderi's lips pursed for a whistle, but
Manawyddan trod on his foot in time, and he was
silent.

"And by then," her voice sobered, "many were
talking of the great woe at Arberth, and of Rhiannon's punishment. Word of it had reached Gwent
that first winter, and Teyrnon and his lady had
looked at each other once, and then looked away
again. But the second year, when those tales kept
coming, they took care not to look at each other.
Indeed, they took great pains not to look at each
other, and each would have liked very much not
to be able to see his or her own thoughts.

"Teyrnon's wife said in her heart, He is the apple of my eye, but he is her flesh. Can I do this to another woman, I who have shared the burden of barrenness with her? But how do I know that he is her flesh—I did not see her give him birth! How can I be sure? And he is the apple of Teyrnon's eye too—Teyrnon who has no son! And Teyrnon fought the Great Arm and saved him; he gave him life at more risk than any blood parents could. Who has a better right to him than Teyrnon?'

"And Teyrnon thought, He is the apple of my wife's eye. How can I ask her who has waited so long to give him up now that she has got him at last? Yet I was Pwyll's man once, and we were friends—the Lordship of Gwent was his gift. But how can I be sure that the boy is his?

"And they both thought, *Rhiannon has conceived once; and whatever her woes are by day, every night she still sits Pwyll in his hall, his honored queen, and when the moon is high they go to bed together. Why should she not bear another child?*

Let her conceive—let her conceive . . .

"But the third winter came, and now Guri was running about and even being lifted onto the back of the young stallion who was, in a way, his twin brother. And still no word came that Queen Rhiannon bore any burden save the weight of any guest boor enough to ride upon her back. Every third or fourth moon that happened, though when such foolish fellows left his court, Pwyll had them followed and set upon and taught more gentlemanly manners. That much he could do for her, he who could not refill her womb.

"And May Eve came again, and Guri's fourth summer. A stranger came then to Teyrnon's house. Tall he was, and his hair was black as night, and his eyes were now gray, now green; they changed like the sea. His clothes were old and worn, but he carried a silver harp with golden strings. And nobody had ever heard a harp played as he played that one, or a tale told as he told it.

"Three nights he played for Teyrnon's household, and on the third night he played a song so sweet that it would have made women in childbed close their eyes in sleep, and wounded men in the sharpest pain forget their pangs and find rest. Every living thing in that house fell asleep; men, women, and children slept; the cats and dogs slept, and even the mice in the walls.

"Only Teyrnon was awake. He sat in his seat, the Lord's seat, with the child Guri asleep beside him, his head on his father's knees. And Teyrnon looked at the bard, and the bard looked at Teyrnon.

" 'Once before, Lord of Gwent,' said the harper, 'you woke while others slept.'

" 'How do you know that?' demanded Teyrnon.

" 'I know many things,' the stranger said, 'and I have not stayed here these three days without feeling your thoughts burn in the night. Yours, and your lady's.'

" 'A man's dreams are his own,' said Teyrnon, 'and no stranger has a right to come creeping into them to watch them, and learn secrets that are not meant for him!' His hand went to his sword.

" 'My rights do not matter,' said the stranger. 'But others have rights that do. Look at that child there.' He pointed to the sleeping Guri. 'Have you ever seen such a likeness between father and son as between that boy there and Pwyll, Prince of Dyved?'

Teyrnon looked down at the child, and his eyes saw what for two winters he had been shutting them against. Saw it too plainly ever to forget again . . .

" 'Look at those eyes,' said the stranger; and as he spoke, Guri's eyes opened. They looked up, in sleepy wonder and trust, at the man he called father. And Teyrnon bowed his head.

" 'They are the eyes of Pwyll,' he said heavily. 'The eyes of Pwyll, my Lord and my friend.'

"Then he looked at the bard again and his face changed; fury twisted it. He sprang up, thrusting Guri behind him. He crouched like a beast about to spring, and his drawn sword flashed in the firelight.

" 'Who are you?' The gleam of his blade was not more deadly than the gleam of his eyes. 'Who are you, and what brought you here? Are you another Thing of the night?'

"But there was no answer; there was nobody there to answer him. He stood alone among the sprawled bodies of his sleep-emptied folk. Even the child Guri was asleep again, tranquil as though he had never waked. Teyrnon gathered him up and went from the hall, and his shoulders were bowed like an old man's.

"In the dark of that same night the Lord of Gwent woke his wife and talked with her. He told what he could no longer tell himself that he did not know. He said, 'It is not right for me to keep a boy that I know to be the son of another man. And it is not right for you either, to keep him, and so let so noble a lady bear such punishment.'

"The woman did not weep or cry. She said only, 'You are right, Lord. Long have I known that we should send the boy home.'

"Then for awhile they both sat silent, and in the dark his hand found hers, and she turned and wept upon his breast. But not stormily; she loved him too well to make his load heavier, and soon her mind turned, like a good housewife's, to what might yet be salvaged from the wreck.

" 'In three ways we shall get good from this business, Lord. Thanks and gifts from the Queen for freeing her from punishment, and thanks from Pwyll for nursing his son and restoring him to him. And if the boy's heart is good—and well you know it is!—he will be our foster-son, and he will do us all the good in his power.'

"Foster-sons come back to visit their foster-parents. He will come back to see us. We will see him sometimes—sometimes—That thought was the only light in her darkness.

"In the morning she packed Guri's things and dressed him in his best and combed his golden curls. Then Teyrnon sat him beside him in his chariot, and together they rode away. Two of Teyrnon's best men rode behind them as escort.

"Evening was near when they came to Arberth. They saw Pwyll's palace, round as the setting sun that turned its thatched roof to gold. Behind it rose the blue rugged heights of our Preseli, cloud-drowned, so that none might tell where mountain ended and sky began. And nearer, lower, yet terrible in its strength, loomed that huge and awful Mound that is called the Gorsedd Arberth, The Home of Mysteries, the tomb of Dyved's earliest King, though no man now remembers his tribe or name. Like the home of all shadows it looked, a blackness in which, even by day, night's own blackness might well take shelter and await its hour . . .

"Before the palace doors, that were wide enough to admit twelve men at once, was set a horse block. Beside that block sat a woman, and the sinking sun made her hair shine like a golden flame.

"She rose as she saw them come. Her face was set like a mask, like something carved by godlike craftsmen beyond the Eastern sea. When she first sat beside that block, she must have had to fight for that carved look, fight as hard as ever warrior fought in battle. But day had followed day, week had followed week, and the moons had grown into years; now it was part of her. She flinched only once; when Teyrnon lifted the child down, and he trotted forward by his father's side.

" 'Lord,' her voice was clear and steady, 'come no farther. I will carry every one of you into the palace on my back.'

"Teyrnon's two burly men stopped in their tracks, then looked down with great interest at their feet. Anywhere but at the lady. But Teyrnon faced her, and she him.

" 'This is my penance, Lord,' her eyes were as

steady as her voice, 'for slaying and eating my own son.'

"She had no doubt that Teyrnon believed her guilty; never once in all those years of her sorrow had he, Pwyll's old comrade, come to see them. That did not matter. She had faced too many men to care what one more thought, but the child—his horror still had power to hurt her. She could not bear to see those young eyes widen; she kept her own fixed, unwaveringly, upon the father's face.

"'Lady,' Teyrnon's deep voice shook, 'never think me such a one. Never will I be carried upon your back.'

"He turned upon his men then, and so fierce was his look that they cowered, although such a ride was the last thing they wanted.

"The child Guri piped up, 'Neither will I be, Lady!' His troubled, friendly eyes regarded her.

"And suddenly Rhiannon laughed. The lost smile of her youth came back, and made that carved face alive and sweet.

"'You are one that I would like to carry!' she said, and swept him up in her arms. All of them went into the palace together.

"Great gladness was with Arberth that night. In that royal hall a royal feast was always spread, but when folk knew that Teyrnon, Lord of Gwent, had come, more oxen died, more fowl were roasted. The best mead and wine, the best silver and gold cups were hunted out, the best cheeses fetched and sliced. In the midst of all Pwyll came home from hunting; when first he heard who had come his face filled with joy, then clouded.

"'Did he—?' That question may have been looked, rather than asked.

"But when his smiling people shook their heads, he came forward with outstretched hands and face beaming like the sun. He greeted Teyrnon and seated him between himself and Rhiannon, and the boy sat between Teyrnon's two men. Often the Queen's eyes sought him there.

"They ate and talked and drank, they drank and talked and ate. Pwyll was eager to hear everything that had happened to his friend, and at last he said, 'That fine mare of yours—that was a queer business. Have you ever been able to keep any of her colts?'

"'I have that,' said Teyrnon. 'Four of them now, all as fine horseflesh as ever you saw. But it was a great battle I had to fight to keep the first of those four.'

"And he told the tale of that night, and of the Arm that had come in the night, and women shuddered and men held their breaths. Guri's eyes grew round; he never had heard the tale before.

"Teyrnon told of his victory, and of how his foe had fled wailing to the Underworld. Then he told of that other cry. Of what he had found beside the door.

"Deep was the silence then; deep as a well. Men stared at each other and dared not speak. Each thought, *It cannot be—it could be—*And Pwyll looked at his lady, and waited for the light that did not come into her face. She thought, *I am dreaming again. I have dreamed so many times. Teyrnon does not mean what we think he means. Soon I will wake again.*

"Teyrnon rose and walked through that dead silence. Up to the child he had called his child. From under his cloak he drew the shining stuff that had wrapped the babe; he put it around Guri and lifted him again, as he had lifted him on that other night. He carried him to Rhiannon and set him in her lap.

" 'Lady, here is your son. Whoever told that tale of your slaying him told a wicked lie. I think that there is none out of all this host here who does not see that this boy is the son of Pwyll. Look at him,' he pointed to his lord, 'and then look at the child.'

"From all there a shout went up, 'It is so!' There was power in Teyrnon in that hour; all saw that likeness, even as he himself had seen it, that night when the stranger bard had faced him in his own hall.

"Only Rhiannon sat in mute wonder, her eyes wide and blank as those of the staring child on her lap. Her arms had closed around him, as any woman's arms will close around a child, but she did not look at him. It was as if she did not dare to look . . .

"But then Pwyll rose and threw his arms around them both, and his eyes were wet. She began to shiver then, to shake all over, as a tree might shake in a great wind. She looked down swiftly into Guri's face and then buried her own in his golden hair.

" 'Oh, my darling, if this is true, then I am delivered from the long fear for you, the long grief!'

"And the wise druid, Pendaran Dyved, came

and said to her, 'Well have you named your son, Lady. Pryderi, son of Pwyll, he shall be called forever.' "*

---

*In old Welsh, "Pryderi" seems to have meant something like "Anxiety" or "Grief."

4

The Son of Llyr Remembers

"She did not tell the tale badly." Pryderi stretched himself luxuriously upon the blanket-covered straw that was their bed. "I think she got most of it right. All but one thing."

"What thing was that?" asked Manawyddan politely. He pulled back the covers that Pryderi's stretching had pulled off them. He hoped that Pryderi would soon be ready to sleep.

"It was what that stranger-bard did. He did not vanish into the air."

"What did he do?" Manawyddan's voice was without interest.

Pryderi frowned. "It is strange. I can still see that sword gleaming in the firelight, as Teyrnon's eyes blazed above it. Ready to flash up and down and then up again, dripping red with the stranger's blood. Almost I could see it happening. And my heart was in my throat, for I loved that bard."

"And did it happen?"

"No. He turned his back on that blade and on those eyes. Without hurry he picked up his harp, and without hurry he walked to the door. He went out through it, and we never saw him again."

"His work was done. He had nothing to stay for."

"But who was he? Where did he go? And where did he come from?"

"Surely it is enough that he was your friend, and your parents' friend."

"Yes, but who *was* he? Sometimes it has seemed to me that you have a look of him, Lord."

The son of Llyr laughed softly. "I am no helper out of Faery, lad."

"Nor was he! My mother's kin never sent her help, only harm."

"Do not put shame on your own blood." Manawyddan spoke sternly. "Folk of whom your mother could have been born never could have sent a monster to steal a newborn child. Remember Gwawl the Bright, Gwawl mad Cludd, to whom her kin would have wedded her. She escaped from Gwawl untouched, yet at a price. His hate will never die."

"I know that story. On the wedding night Gwawl came and tricked my father into giving my mother up to him unknowingly. To get away from him, Mother had to trick him into a bag, and then Father and his men each gave that bag a good hard whack with a good stout stick. Until Gwawl promised to release Mother and to take no revenge. By the awful, unnameable oath he swore— it that can blast even a God if he breaks it. Gwawl sent no monsters."

"Yet Gwawl had friends whom no oath bound. Had it not been for Arawn, King of Annwn, your father's own friend in Faery, all Dyved would have been blasted long ago. Surely you know that, lad."

"But if those powers dared not touch Pwyll, how could they have dared to touch me, his son? Unless they were of my kin on the mother's side, and so had a claim on me that even mighty Arawn must respect?"

Manawyddan said, "We cannot fathom the ways of the Otherworld, lad, we who are mortal men. Let us sleep."

But when they had settled themselves for that sleep, he thought, *Almost you tore the veil from more than secret tonight, Pryderi. But this you never have suspected, and never shall suspect: that no drop of Pwyll's blood flows in your veins.*

That night had been as dark as this. Softly and quietly the moon had risen through cloudy darknesses, higher and yet higher, moving ever westward across the unthinkable vastness of heaven. In her pale light Pwyll, Prince of Dyved, had sat drinking with his guest, and both men had watched her gleaming roundness, so much gentler than the sun's.

"Nine more moons we have—Rhiannon and I. Nine only." Pwyll's voice was rough with pain.

"That could be time enough. Do not waste it."

"We have done all we can. We have lain together beneath each Stone of the Holy Stones, and done every rite the druids advised. We have done every foolish thing the old wives tell of. And nothing has happened. As I knew that nothing would happen."

He laughed harshly, bitterly, his face twisting.

In puzzled pity the other man sat and watched him.

Pwyll recovered himself, turned to him and smiled, "But now I do waste time. There is one way left. The Gods must have sent you here, son of Llyr, brother of Bran my Overlord."

Manawyddan said slowly, "You mean the visiting overlord's right to sleep with his host's wife? That is not the way of the Old Tribes. Bran never would claim it. Nor will I."

Pwyll still smiled. "If Rhiannon were a mother, I would be glad indeed of your forbearance; I own that. But she is not, and the custom is old among the New Tribes, and it has good in it. The King is always supposed to be the best man in the Tribe, the strongest and the most skillful. And the more women he sleeps with the more sons he begets, so the stronger the Tribe is."

Manawyddan said grimly, "If I loved a woman and she me, any other man that went to bed with her would indeed have to be stronger than I." His face was hard; he was thinking of his own mother, dark Penardim, and of how to ransom his father Llyr, captured by treachery, she had had to submit her body to the captor and to bear the twins Nissyen and Evnissyen, those two who were unlike any other men ever born on the Island of the Mighty.

Pwyll said, "Shame is in what a man thinks it is in." His face was cold now; like a carven image.

"That is often the truth. But seldom is any saying true always." Manawyddan brooded. When first he had seen Rhiannon he had thought her the fairest of women; when they had talked together,

he had known that their minds flowed in the same
channels, that the same things would move them
to laughter or pity. But also he had known that
she loved his friend. Not until now, when the cup
of cups was offered him, with no wine in it to
slake his thirst, had he known the fierceness of
that thirst. Yet the heat of his blood whispered in
spite of him, *Yet you would have her. Touch her
—hold her . . .*

He said violently, "Among the Old Tribes no
woman sleeps with a man unless she wants him.
Otherwise her child would be born outside the
Ancient Harmonies, against the will of the Mothers. I will not beget such a child—nor would you
want me to if you knew my brother Evnissyen.
Get your own children, man!"

Pwyll's eyes met his steadily. "I cannot."

For a breath's space cold silence fell; then
Manawyddan thrust back understanding. "If your
Queen's own people have made her barren, my
seed will not take root in her either. Why do this
ill deed for nothing?"

Pwyll said, "You have heard that in my youth I
went into Faery to fight for Arawn, King of
Annwn. To kill for him that terrible foe who
would have wrested Annwn from him, and so
have changed the course of our own world also."

"You did a great deed."

"And great has been its price. Those Shadow-
folk needed earth-strength to fight the White
Shadow—him who had brought bloody death even
into their world. And only from an earth-man
could they get it, violence being the element we
are born to. But the man who has so used his

strength cannot bring it all back to earth. He who has touched so much death must die a little. Leave something of himself behind, among the Shadows ..."

"You brought back strength enough. I know that, who have seen you on the battlefield—" Manawyddan stopped and bit his lip. Too late he understood. Meeting those still steady eyes, the depth of pain and shame in them, he felt such horror as only a strong man can feel at sight of another strong man maimed. *He minds this more than I would mind the loss of my right hand, or one of the legs I stand on. He is ashamed, too; as only cowardice should shame a man ...*

The son of Llyr had this virtue: he could pity with all his heart what seemed to him folly. No man should feel lessened by what he could not help; by a lack or a difference from other men. But if he did ...

Pwyll said quietly, "Rhiannon knows. I could not let her blame herself. Being a woman, she is still noble enough or foolish enough to love me. Now we three know. And I know your honor too well, son of Llyr, to say to you, let there never be a fourth."

Manawyddan thought swiftly, *But you have let your people blame her—Rhiannon.* And then as swiftly, *But you are not like Bran and me. You have no brother, no near kinsman—they have only you to turn to. And if they knew this—they who know your courage and your nobleness best of all—they would lose faith in you. Mill about like leaderless beasts afraid of wolves. That is what your knowledge has done for you, you men of the*

*New Tribes, who are so proud of being fathers.
We of the Old Tribes judge a man by his own
worth, not by what his seed can do inside a woman's womb.*

Aloud he said, "I will do my best for you, Lord
of Dyved. I will use the druid power that my
House has, but seldom uses—I will put on your
shape, so that Rhiannon will think that it is still
yourself she lies with."

Pwyll smiled. "Yet I doubt if you could fool her
all night long . . . "

"I know. And I will not ask what love words
you two use together—those no third person ever
should know. Go to her and tell her—I suppose
she does know of this pretty plan of yours, does
she not?"

"She does. She is a great lady. She said, 'When I
came to you I accepted the way of your people.
Tell the son of Llyr that I will welcome him as
the mother of his son should.' "

"Yet I would not have her nobly endure me.
Tell her that from tonight until I leave, you and
she must not speak together in the night. So she
will not know when I come to her."

Pwyll said with grave dignity, "Lord, I thank
you."

When he went to Rhiannon his wife, he told
her what their friend and guest had said. She
laughed—a laugh that was half a sob—flung her
arms around him and held him close.

"That is like his nobleness! I was afraid—I can
tell you that now, Lord. I was afraid. To lie with
any man but you—" She kissed him long and hard.

When he turned from her to take off his clothes,

the shadows were thick about him. Had her mind been calmer she, the woman out of Faery, would have known that one of those shadows was a man.

His bare feet made no sound on the rushes as he left that quiet, moonlit room; left her. She was not listening; she was only waiting. Seeing, with what relief and happiness, the dear, familiar head turn back to her, the dear, familiar body advance upon her. "Whatever happens tomorrow night, tonight, Lord, we are still together!"

To Manawyddan her white face and outstretched arms, the sweet loveliness of her two white breasts, still looked like things of Faery . . .

Now, lying awake beside his son and hers, he thought, *It was well done. She never dreamed that we would change places in the very hour that Pwyll spoke with her. The boy was begotten as the Ancient Harmonies would have all children begotten: in shared love and desire.*

Yet soon fresh trouble had come. The dread Otherworldly foes had proved their reality, snatching away the newborn life. He remembered the long misery, knowing what *her* fear and misery and shame must be. Remembered the long peering into that shining dish of clear water; water in which the druid-trained could see what was far away. Striving to keep his mind away from her face, from that accursed horse block—to find that other face, that unknown baby face that might be nowhere on earth. Again and again he had seen Teyrnon's house in the water; at last he had found it upon earth. It, and the sturdy little son he had never seen. The joy of that hour had been his own, if nothing else ever could be. A pity that it had had to end the joy of others . . .

You owe much to Teyrnon, lad; as much as any boy could ever owe his own father, maybe more. He fought a great fight for you on your birth night, but maybe the fight he fought with himself, later, was harder. He would have won that one too, by himself, if I had not hurried him. But whatever I did was good if it saved her one day by that horse block.

He had sent her boy home to her. He had helped Teyrnon to conquer himself; ironically in the event, he had even conquered Another, that unseen, unknown Might of whose terribleness that monster had been only the servant . . .

Or had he? Suddenly in that darkness Eyes met his, those same Eyes that he had felt watching them the day before. Eyes sea-gray as his own, but colder, deeper than the sea. Cold with the cold of vast and unfathomable space. *Look. Look and know your littleness. None can conquer Me. I am beyond age and death. To Me one of your lifetimes is less than half the passing of a moon. Though I wait a few breaths' space of My time to strike, still the blow will fall. And beneath it all you miserable mites will shriek and flee and be crushed into nothingness.*

That Voice that made no sound chilled Manawyddan's heart. He sank into a darkness that seemed to be that threatened nothingness.

5

Homecoming

In the dewy sweetness of the dawn they set out again. The way was hard and rough, straight up through those dark mountains that cradled the Holy Stones. But Pryderi sang as he went. His eyes shone like the sun that soon beat down hot upon them.

"Before nightfall we shall be home, Lord. *Home!*"

Your home, Manawyddan thought. *Will any place on earth ever again be home to me?* Well, nothing must dampen the boy's happiness; nothing must spoil this day for him. He trudged along unhappily. A black mood was on him; he could not understand how he could have been such a fool as to let himself be trapped into seeing Rhiannon again. To come as a beggar before her who was still a queen—what part was that for a proud man? For any man? Better far to have let her remember him as she always had; as one who had helped her in need, then had too much delicacy ever again to inflict his presence upon her. He had been the High King's brother when last they met, he who was now a landless wanderer, kinless and friendless forever.

No—not quite friendless. He could not escape

the boy's hospitality now, whatever craziness had been on him when he accepted it.

He had been needed in Dyved once. Now he was not needed anywhere . . .

I dreamed something last night. What was it? Like a black wing, memory brushed him, and was gone.

Sunset was past when they saw the Gorsedd Arberth, that mighty Mound that all men feared. Flowers grew there, but no child ever plucked them. Gold might well be buried there, with that once great, now nameless King, but no robber was fool enough to seek it. Many generations of lords and warriors had avoided that Mound, as men avoid a bed of hot coals. Only in evil times, when trouble threatened the whole Tribe, had a few Princes of Dyved gone up there, daring death. The King who mounted that Mound was beaten to death, or else he saw a wonder. . .

Pwyll had seen a wonder. He had sat upon that Mound and seen its side open to let Rhiannon ride out, upon a white horse and clad in a golden gown. The Holy Bride meant for him. . .

But now that fabled Mound was quiet, purple in the gray evening, and as they drew nearer they saw smoke curling against its grim heights, and then the palace huddled below it, the palace where Pryderi had been born.

Pryderi gave a great shout of joy. "We are here! Here!" And sped forward, too lost in his gladness to notice Manawyddan's silence.

The great doors yawned before them, as once long ago they had yawned before Teyrnon and the little Guri. The doorkeeper saw them, saw Pryderi, and stared; stared again, then rushed inside. Men and women came swarming out, like bees out of a hive, all shouting together, "Lord! Lord Pryderi!"

Like bees they swarmed upon him, all trying to kiss his hands, his clothes, any part of him they could reach.

Then two more women came, and before them all fell back; opened a lane that led straight to him.

One hesitated, till she saw his face, then cried out and came running. She was young and tall and deep-bosomed, apple-sound and honey-sweet: Kigva, the daughter of Gwynn Gloyu. She flung herself upon Pryderi, and they hugged and kissed each other as though trying to squeeze themselves into one body, to do away with all separateness and all chance of any more separation forever.

The other woman came more slowly. But her eyes drank in Pryderi with a joy as warm, as enfolding, as touch. Time had clawed with graying fingers at the gold of her hair, had tramped across her face and left tiny footprints around eyes and mouth, but her beauty shone on through the aging flesh, as the light shines through an alabaster lamp.

She saw Manawyddan, and her eyes lit for him. For himself, not merely for her guest. She came to him.

"A welcome is with you here, son of Llyr! Long has it been since you came to this house, though there is no man we could be as glad to see, save my son himself!"

He took her outstretched hands, and by some magic he was no longer embarrassed or ashamed.

They went inside, and the feast was spread before them, the feast that perhaps Rhiannon's Birds had told her to have ready. Kigva sat next to Pryderi, but Rhiannon put Manawyddan between her son and herself. And the son of Llyr could no more look away from her than Pryderi could look away from Kigva. The turn of her head, the lifting of her hand, the shape of her mouth as she spoke each new thought, all these were music. Each brought her some new form of loveliness that he thought could not be bettered, and then she would move again, and the new sight ravish him anew with fresh beauty.

He thought, *She is as beautiful as she ever was. She is more beautiful than she ever was. She has a grace that makes youth seem boisterous and crude.*

But Pryderi and Kigva were well satisfied with their youth. To each it seemed that nothing could possibly be so fine and wonderful as the other. They laughed and talked and ate together— Pryderi ate a great deal—yet their eyes never left each other. And as the night wore, they talked less, and Kigva ceased to eat and drink at all.

At last the time came they longed for. The feast was over, and the young King and Queen went to bed together. Rhiannon went to her own sleeping-place, and Manawyddan lay down in the one given him. Yet his closed eyes still saw Rhiannon.

So it was for the next night, and the next. The nobles of Dyved kept pouring in to welcome Pryderi home, and since those who had hoped to get his throne had to take care to shout their gladness as loudly as those who really felt it (often they shouted louder), there was never a moment's quiet. During those three days any man in that palace at Arberth would have been hard put to it to hear himself think.

Yet Manawyddan and Rhiannon talked together, and heard only each other. Their minds and their voices flowed together, as the voice and the harp of the bard flow together. And the longer Manawyddan looked at her and talked with her, the more it seemed to him that that far-sung beauty of the Queen of Dyved was sweeter and more comfortable now in her fading than it had been in her bright youth. She too had lost, and had wept for her dead. In her too, as in him, were barren places that never would blossom again, and where she too must always be alone.

Yet she lived, as he lived, and she was lonely, as he was lonely . . .

And on the last night of the feast, when the moon was well on her westward road, he said to the young Lord of Dyved, "Pryderi, I would be glad indeed for it to be as you said."

"What was it he said?" asked Rhiannon, and though her voice was curious, her mouth was not. It had all knowledge, that mouth; it was sweet, and a little wicked too.

Pryderi looked at her and cleared his throat, then cleared it again. He had been too busy with his own affairs to see how things were shaping between his mother and his friend, and here, under her eye, his offer did not sound quite as it had when he had made it to Manawyddan. He had

been sure then that she would gladly do that or
anything else to please him—she always had,
whenever she had felt that the thing in question
would not be bad for him (a point on which, in his
early youth, they had sometimes differed). But
now he was suddenly aware that he had taken a
good deal upon himself.

"Lady," he said, and cleared his throat yet
again. "Lady, I offered you as a bride to the son of
Llyr. Indeed," he rushed on before she could
speak, "there is no finer man alive than he is, and
when I said it I thought I would be doing good to
both of you. Indeed and in very deed"—here he
grinned at her as radiantly as he had when he was
small and she had caught him doing something
that he was fairly sure she would not want him to
do—"I still think I am. If you will let me,
Mother."

Then Rhiannon's smile opened fully, like a
scarlet flower in the sun. "You have said it, and
glad will I be to abide by your saying, Son."

In the morning Manawyddan awoke beside
Rhiannon. He lay there beside her and looked at
her, and it seemed to him that he felt life itself
lapping about him in that chamber, lapping him
like a warm sea. Life as surely as if it had been
youth renewed, the rapture of the sun rising in
the scarlet east, not the earth-fed strength of
storm-blasted trees healing and thrusting forth
new branches.

Not reborn, scarred but still growing, up and
on—on . . .

Then he saw that she was watching him

through her lashes, a quiet twinkle in her eyes, and he smiled.

"Good morning to you, Lady."

She smiled back and stretched herself as a cat stretches. "It is a good morning. The best morning that either of us has known for a long time. Did you truly think, Lord, that you and that overgrown child of mine could keep any secrets from me? That I had not thought of this and willed it, long before my boy thought of it and willed it?"

"Never, Lady. I feared that you had loved Pwyll too much ever to be willing to take another man."

She sobered. "I loved Pwyll, and I love him. But he is gone, so here on earth there is nothing I can do with that love. When my own son offered me to you, when my Bird flew over you, and the golden feather dropped at your feet, did you not hear my call?"

"I thought I dreamed, Lady. Out of my own longing, childishly."

She laughed softly; a tender, mocking laugh, and rubbed her face against his. "True it is, as they say: You are no claimant of lands or possessions, Manawyddan."

"I find myself enough to master, Lady. Without struggling greedily for mastery over things that perhaps should not belong to me."

"None will call you greedy, Lord. You will always let Caswallon wear your crown—and well I know why, who would hate as much as you to see this island bathed in blood! You will never even claim the son you yourself begot. And with all my heart I thank you for that, who know how much it meant to Pwyll to have Pryderi think him his father."

"He is ill-bred who takes back the gift he has given. I have wondered, Lady: did you ever guess on which night the boy was begotten?"

She laughed again and drew his head to her breast. "I knew. Not for awhile, but before the night was over. I knew that the man I lay with loved me—that I was not being taken like some rare dish a host sets before his guest—but there was a difference. So when you slept, I put your own shape back upon you for a moment to make sure—some little tricks I still know, who had to leave most of my powers behind me in the Bright World."

"I am sorry. I thought I had put no grief or shame on you."

"You did not. At the time I would have been better pleased if I could have felt a little grief or shame. Shame—" she sobered again. "You did the deed generously and with great delicacy, Lord; a deed that another might have made horrible. When it would have been betrayal to love and blasphemy not to love, you did your best to spare me both evils. For that, as well as for my son himself, I long have wanted to thank you."

"You owe me no thanks." His eyes twinkled. "That was the best night of my youth, Lady. It could have been better only had it been myself you loved and chose."

"I love you now." She put her arms round his neck.

Two more such nights they had. The third night was that of full moon, and toward morning laughter wakened them. Laughter coming from the other side of the wall, where Kigva and Pryderi had their bed. That new-fangled luxury, a window, had been cut in the outer wall there, and evidently the two young people were looking out of it.

Kigva said, "Look at the moon, Lord! Was it ever so round and fair before? Even now, when it is setting."

Pryderi answered, "It is two moons I see, on a white sky—rare the sight! Let me see if I am seeing double, Lady, or if they are really there."

Then silence, and then Kigva laughing, "It is to feel you meant, not to see—" and sounds that might have been whispers, but most likely were kissing, there in the morning dusk.

Rhiannon smiled. "We must have a window cut in here too, Lord. For years after I lost Pwyll I wanted to shut myself into the dark. It used to make me sad to hear those two children being happy, even while I was glad for them. When I lay here alone."

Manawyddan gathered her into his arms. "Lady, long will it be before you lie alone again!"

Yet that time was to come sooner than either of them dreamed.

That morning restlessness was on Pryderi. For one flashing second, when he saw his mother coming to the breakfast table, Manwyddan's arm around her, it lit up with the old loving mischief. But before and after that it was as heavy as the body of a pregnant woman near her time.

He fidgeted. His hands seemed to want to do something, yet to be dissatisfied with anything they undertook. His feet seemed to want to go somewhere, yet to be unwilling to lift him from his seat.

He did not eat. He only nibbled at his food and then threw it away, and nothing could have been more unlike Pryderi than that.

Kigva and Manawyddan sat and watched him, in worried wonder. Rhiannon sat and watched him awhile, then spoke.

"Son, it is a new face you have on, and I liked the old one better."

Pryderi threw back his head and looked at her defiantly. "I do not like it either, and soon I am going to have to do something that we will both like less. For that Caswallon Mab Beli, who calls himself High King now, will soon hear that I am at home, if he has not heard it already, and if I do not go to him and pay him homage, he will get suspicious of me and maybe come after it."

He stopped and glared at his mother, as if that were her fault, and when she looked back at him unmoved, he glared at the ceiling.

"I do not know what to do except to go and give it to him, and if one must drink sour milk there is no use in putting it off."

He stopped again and looked very hard at the floors and the walls and the ceiling. He carefully looked anywhere and everywhere except at those three he loved best.

He was afraid, desperately afraid of what they might be thinking of him. Manawyddan, his rightful King, to whom this paying of homage to the usurper might well seem both cowardice and treachery. His mother, now rightful Queen over all the Island of the Mighty, who might well see things in the same light. And Kigva—Kigva, who had always thought him the bravest and strongest of men. Able to tread all foes beneath his feet.

He waited for them to speak out, in a chorus of amazed horror and wrath. He waited for them to be silent, and their silence was what he thought most likely, and feared the most.

What did happen startled him as nothing else on earth could have done. Rhiannon took up a bit of meat and remarked calmly and casually, yet with admiration in her tone, "Son, you are growing up."

Manawyddan said, "It is the only thing you can do. Dyved cannot stand alone against all the rest of the Island of the Mighty, and by bringing me here you must already have roused Caswallon's suspicions. You are right—the sooner you go to him the better."

"There is no such hurry on him as that." Rhiannon swallowed her meat hastily, then turned to her son. "Indeed, Lord and dear, Caswallon is in Kent, as either of you two men would have known if you had bothered to ask questions. Wait until he is nearer: do not seem too eager. And there is this good in sour milk: it always keeps."

"It does," said Pryderi, greatly impressed. He sighed with relief and leaned back in his chair; then saw his breakfast, and went to work on it with great vigor.

He was brave. For himself, he would gladly have fought that usurping magician-king, for all his power to slay invisibly. He did not admire common sense, any more than any young man admires an ugly woman, but now he could not sacrifice himself without sacrificing other people, indeed all Dyved. So, since protecting them meant ceasing to admire himself, his plan, unheroic as he thought it, was probably the most heroic deed of his life.

But Rhiannon was troubled. That night she talked with Manawyddan. "We must not let him go to Caswallon too soon, Lord. Not until you have had time to school him. For Pryderi cannot think any way but straight, and Caswallon, who cannot think straight, will not understand him. All could so easily go wrong!"

Manawyddan put his arm about her. "Be at ease, Lady. Caswallon will not slay a guest. That would be worse than his old blood-guiltiness that folk are just beginning to forget."

"But accidents can be arranged! Poison . . ."

"Who would give Caswallon the benefit of the doubt? A name once smeared is never really clean again. And I think that Caswallon will be truly glad to see the boy. Peace is what he wants and needs now, most of all."

Yet on him too there was fear. Discretion was a new growth in the young Lord of Dyved; that morning it had shown itself, but it still could be but a young and tender plant. Caswallon's own discretion should be dependable, yet constant strain and watchfulness tell upon a man. Blood-guilt, even smothered, unacknowledged pangs of conscience, may well drive him to shed more blood. And there was one danger that Rhiannon must never guess. If Caswallon suspected the secret of Pryderi's birth, saw in him a rival—there had been talk, if only guesswork and whispers. He remembered Branwen's gentle mocking, long ago.

He said, slowly, "Perhaps I should go with Pryderi. I offer my own homage."

"And thrust your own head into the wolf's mouth too? No. With you here, Caswallon will know that if he harms Pryderi, Dyved will not be left headless. Men from all of the parts of the Island of the Mighty would flock to you then. Not all men, but many."

Manawyddan chuckled. "So then it is safe for Pryderi to go. You yourself disprove all your fears."

"It is not as simple as that, and you know it! You are afraid too. Let us think . . . "

They talked much, and thought long.

Old Pendaran Dyved's dying won them some delay. He had lived only for Pryderi's homecoming, he who long had guarded queens and realm as best he could. But it was Manawyddan, not Pryderi, he asked to talk with at the last.

"I am glad to shift my load to your shoulders, son of Llyr. You may think you have borne loads enough, but the truth is that you are a man born to carry loads. Free, your eyes lose their sparkle and your shoulders slump."

"You are wise, old man. Wiser than I thought."

The old druid smiled. "You never thought me wise. And I know why: I knew why of old, when I was a guest at Harlech. As I fear another knew too."

"I was always courteous to you . . . "

"And no more. There is no time left for anything but truth between us, brother of Bran the Blessed."

Old wrath and old pain boiled up in Manawyddan. For what his sister had suffered in Ireland, for what Rhiannon had suffered here.

"Never would druids of the Old Tribes have let their Queen or any other woman be used like a she-ass—made to carry men on her back! Worse—to be made to keep telling and retelling those other women's hideous lies, accusing herself of such foulness! Their eyes would have pierced the lies— have made the liars blubber and wail for mercy. Pwyll was no Matholuch; only a decent man, striving to do his best for both his wife and his people. But you druids—I know your wisdom and your goodness, Pendaran Dyved, many times since then they have been proved, but never will I understand what was on you then!"

The old face grew grave. "I had no wisdom to strive against what menaced Dyved then, Lord. We druids here were all helpless: we looked into the water and the crystal, and we could see nothing but clouds. Only the Grayness—the Grayness. It had Eyes. Only I ever saw those Eyes." His face twisted; he gasped. "They came to me in the night. Their evil entered into me; made me mock her and give the most brutal sentence that we dared give, Lord. For the fear of Pwyll was on us too. But those Eyes . . ."

He struggled for breath. Manawyddan said gently, "Peace be with you, Pendaran Dyved. If you failed Rhiannon once, since then you have guarded her long and well. I grieve that I reminded you of what is over and done."

"It is not over! He—waits. Watch well, son of Llyr!"

The dying man cried aloud those words, his last. He spoke no more, though through two more nights he breathed.

Then he died and was mounded, and many mourned for him, Rhiannon the Queen not least. And a week later Pryderi set out for the Court of Caswallon. Nobly he went, dressed in his best, with the finest young men he had left around him. Golden ornaments glittered on his crimson cloak, and even on the trappings of his white horse, the finest of stallions, that was a grandson to the foal that Teyrnon had saved along with him, on that dread night long ago.

But Manawyddan watched him go, his heart cold with dread. For he was remembering those words of Pendaran Dyved's: "*. . . at Harlech. As I fear another knew too.*" What meaning could they have had except that Caswallon had scented out the secret of Pryderi's birth?

6

Before Caswallon

The young lord of Dyved and his train were but a half day's journey from the house where Caswallon was, when a strange man met them on the road.

He was tall and old, and his ragged clothes were of as many colors as the rainbow. Over one shoulder he bore a dilapidated bag of hide, with most of the hair worn off it. But over the other hung a golden harp with silver strings.

He said, "Lord, may I travel with you?"

Some of Pryderi's young men looked insulted, and all looked surprised, but Pryderi stared hard at the stranger.

"Man," he said, "have I not seen you before?"

"Lord, I have sung in the halls of many chiefs. Maybe I sang in your father's, and you small."

"My father was Pwyll, Prince of Dyved."

"A noble man, and a far-famed. I sang in his palace at Arberth once, before he had a son."

Pryderi hesitated, trying not to be seen looking at the stranger's clothes. "I would like well to hear any bard that sang for my father, but now I am on my way to see the High King. If you will turn back to Arberth, my mother and my wife will give you good welcome there. I will soon be home again."

He thought that shabby man would shrink from facing all the fine bards of Caswallon's Court, but to his surprise the stranger said, "I would rather go with you now, Lord. If I may."

"Come then," said Pryderi. He turned to the man who had charge of his baggage. "Get him a cloak."

But the stranger shook his head. "You are generous, Lord, as is to be expected of your father's son. But these clothes and I are old comrades; we will not part now."

"Let it be as you please," said Pryderi.

So the stranger fared with them, and they all fared on, and before sunset they came to the place where the King was. It was a place of druidcraft, of wise men and teachers; later, men were to call it Oxford. Caswallon, once the pupil only of magicians, lately had turned to the study of the higher wisdom. He wanted to wipe out memory of his kingship's bloody beginnings, to be remembered as Beli his father still was, for nobleness as well as power.

He gave Pryderi a great welcome, and he and all his men made much of him. "I call this finely done of you, young Lord," he said, "you who were such great friends with my cousins, to come in so soon and wish me joy of my kingship."

"You are the King," said Pryderi, "and this island needs peace. May it be as blessed under you, as once it was under Bran."

That was all he could bring himself to say, and he nearly choked on it, but Caswallon shook his hand and laughed.

Deep into the night they made merry. Then

Caswallon said, "I have one thing to ask of you, young Lord. Give it me and I will ask no tribute of Dyved again so long as you live."

Pryderi sat up sharply, the wine fumes clearing from his head. He thought in horror, *What if he means to ask me for Manawyddan's head?* He said aloud, his eyes fixing Caswallon's, "Ask what you will, Lord. So long as it is honorable for me to give, I will give it."

Again Caswallon laughed. "I see that you have not forgotten that other feast, your parents' wedding feast, when Gwawl the Bright came in disguise and asked a boon. When your father granted the gift but forgot to set limits to it, and Gwawl asked for the bride herself."

"But Gwawl got nothing by that slip of my father's. Nothing but shame and stripes." Pryderi's eyes still pinned Caswallon's. In the shadows behind them one or two men gasped.

But Caswallon still smiled. "Your chiefs hold meetings and your druids rites in an ancient Ring of Holy Stones. To you New Tribes, it is spoil of war; your grandfathers' grandfathers never set eyes on it. But to the Old Tribes it is holy indeed; nothing that men can see or touch could be holier."

"To my people too it is holy." Pryderi was breathing more easily now, but his eyes looked puzzled. "Four generations of us have worshipped and held our councils there. We do no mockery or sacrilege against it."

"None says you do. But the wise men with me here—some of them druids who have served Beli my father as well as Bran my cousin—say that they know a place in which those God-Stones could sit and bring man such wisdom as he never yet has had. Where they could watch and time the ceaseless marching of the great Stars that walk through the sky like men—yes, and even foretell the coming of that great Darkness that sometimes swallows up sun and moon."

Pryderi said slowly, "My people would not like to give up the Holy Ring. Nor do I see how it could be moved."

"I say that it could be moved."

Pryderi was silent awhile; then he said, "This is a great matter. I must speak of it with my chieftains and my druids in the Ring itself. Those God-Stones are holy to all the men of Dyved. They are not the King's nor any man's to give away."

"A King speaks for his people," said Caswallon.

"A war-king does, in time of war. Not so the Lord of peaceful folk, in time of peace."

"To have their taxes eased soothes all men." Caswallon grinned.

But Pryderi stuck to what he had said, though the King pressed him. At last, maybe partly to ease that pressure, he asked questions about where the Stones were to go, and when he heard he laughed.

"For a bird in flight that would be a long journey. And stones are not birds—they do not fly. Come and get them if you can."

"Is that a bargain?" Caswallon's eyes were keen.

Pryderi laughed again. "It is, Lord. And if the Stones make themselves light as feathers and fly away with you, then indeed my people and I will know that it is the Gods' will that they go. For you could never carry them half that far."

"The Gods will help us," said Caswallon, "for it is Their will. And Their blessing will be upon you."

He held out his hand and Pryderi took it and grinned. "Yet meaning no disrespect to Them or you, Lord, I fear that Dyved will be paying you tribute this year and next, and for many a year to come."

Caswallon grinned back. "We shall see." But within himself he had ceased to laugh. He thought, *This young man is stiff-necked, if a little simple. It is well for a stiff neck to have no head on top of it.*

Next morning the feasters slept late; all but the stranger who had come with Pryderi. He rose early and went down to a stream near the house; he washed his face and hands there, and the wind blew cool and sweet in his face.

He looked about him, and saw that the land was green and gentle, and what else he saw in it only druid-bred eyes could know. He said to himself, *This is a place for birth. Not for the births of the body, but one where knowledge will be worshipped, and great thoughts born. By listening to its druids, Caswallon may achieve memorable deeds, but he will not do them for the people's sake, or for their own goodness. He will do them for his own pride and power. He has not changed.*

He lay down on those green grasses in whose place so many walls and roofs were to rise, roofs beneath which so much thinking was to be done, and he thought.

*At first Caswallon was glad to see the boy. His
mind was not made up. Not until he saw that the
lad had manhood in him. That could be dangerous in any man who still loved the House of Bran.
But most dangerous of all in the son of Manawyddan son of Llyr."*

But if Caswallon had any inkling of that secret,
as yet he had given no sign of it. Eyes that last
night had watched the mind behind his face—the
trained mind that could be almost, but not quite,
as well guarded as that face—had found nothing.

The day wore. By twos and threes the feasters
woke and straggled out into the sun. Some of
them had headaches, and some of them had belly-
aches, and some of them had both, but when the
women brought out breakfast many of the young
men still had good appeties after all. Pryderi had,
and Caswallon sat beside him and made as much
of him as he had the night before. Drink never
turned Caswallon's head.

The King had almost finished his breakfast
when his eye lit upon the tall shabby man who
stood among Pryderi's men. His eyes met the
stranger's eyes, and their gray directness puzzled
him. For a breath's space memory flickered
through his mind then away again, as a moth or a
gnat flicks past a man's face.

He said, "Pryderi, who is that tall fellow with
the harp? He is not dressed like your other men."

Pryderi laughed. "That is a tactful way of putting it, Lord. He joined me yesterday. I offered
him a new cloak, but he would not take it."

The King frowned. "That is a queer way for a

beggar to act. Usually they grab at whatever they can get."

Pryderi said, a trifle stiffly, "He is no beggar, Lord. See, his harp is fine."

"Can he use it, I wonder? Here, fellow, come and give us a tune."

The stranger came up to their table then, and played for them, and no man or woman there ever had heard music that was sweeter.

When he had finished, Caswallon drew a deep breath. "Man, you are the king of harpers!"

The stranger said, "Some men are kings of one thing, Lord, some of another."

Caswallon's face changed; for a breath's space his eyes grew hard. Then he took the fine gold chain from about his own neck and threw it to the harper. The bard had to stoop to pick it up, and Pryderi, without knowing how he knew it, suddenly understood that this was what the High King had wanted—to make that straight back stoop and that high head bow to pick up his gift from the dust. To show all men what kind of kingship mattered, how little an artist's gifts and skills counted beside place and power.

But why? Pryderi thought, his mouth stiff with distaste. *Why should he care?*

But the stranger straightened, his brow unruffled, even a faint amusement in his eyes. He walked toward Caswallon, chain in hand.

"Such a gift is too great a treasure, Lord King, for a poor wandering man of the roads. Never could I close my eyes without fear that in my sleep some other man would cut my throat to get it.

And some night some man would." He held out the chain to Caswallon.

The King said, "Your wanderings are over." He paused, and that pause seemed, strangely, to darken the morning sun. Then he added, his voice silken soft, "You shall stay with me always, and play that sweet music of yours for me every night."

"Lord, I could not hope to please so great a King for long. Some days my music is sweet, others it is sour."

"It is not every man that is offered the place of bard to the High King. Suppose I do not let you go, fool?" Caswallon's voice was low, but his eyes burned like hot coals.

The stranger said easily, "You will do according to your kind of kingcraft, Lord, as I will do according to mine. Would you like me to do tricks for you? I am a cunning man, as well as a musician."

Some stiffness, some dread that had been in the air, went out of it. People relaxed; some smiled. The harping-man had sense; he was going to give in, after all. But Caswallon's eyes did not soften, though their light grew cold.

"Well, fellow, show us what you can do."

The chain still swung from the stranger's hand. He laid it down on the table beside Caswallon, took down his own worn bag from his shoulder, and held that high.

"This little bag cannot hold much. Bear witness to that, all men."

He set it down and untied its mouth. He took out a ball of silver thread that glistened, moon-bright, in the sun. One of Pryderi's men whispered to him, "Small as that bag is, it could hold a hundred balls like that. I am afraid this is not going to be much good."

"Wait and see what he does with it," Pryderi whispered back.

Shielding his eyes with his hand, the stranger looked up at the sky. It was blue, bluer than the deepest sea, yet here and there white clouds floated upon it, delicate huge masses that looked heavenly soft, yet solid as the thatched roof below. Whitenesses with curly edges that grew ever thinner and finer until they melted into that depth of blueness and were lost.

The stranger spun the ball round in his hand. He spun it round and round. It shone brighter than silver ever could. It grew bigger and brighter. It shone brighter than the moon. It shone like the sun's very self.

All eyes were fixed upon the spinning brightness. Not one could have looked away even though a spear or an arrow had flashed towards that person from beneath that glowing, spinning ball.

A length of thread came loose from that ball. It did not fall earthward, or float upon the wind, as even the finest thread should have done. It darted straight up, like a bird.

Up and up and up it went, higher than any bird ever flew. They should no longer have been able to see its upper part, but still they saw its whole length, stretching from earth to heaven.

It came to a cloud, it wrapped itself around and

around that cloud; became a shining bridge, fine as a hair.

"So far, so good," said the stranger.

He stooped to his bag again, put the ball back inside, and took out a white hare much too big to have been in there.

"Up, hare!" he said, and set it down facing the thread. And though any of its paws was many times wider than that narrowest of bridges, it sped upward without any trouble at all. Up and up, through the sky, until it reached the cloud, and was lost in that whiteness so like its whiteness.

All gasped but the bard. He stooped and took a small snow-white hound out of the bag. He set it on its feet and said, "Dog, go after that hare."

And the dog ran up the thread as the hare had done.

It too vanished, and soon the wild sweet music of its belling came drifting down from heaven. They knew that it must be chasing the hare through the clouds.

Again the bard stooped to his bag. This time he seemed to have trouble in getting out what was inside. A head came finally, the curly yellow head of a boy in his teens, and a woman screamed. But a chest followed the head, and then long legs that carried the rest. The whole boy stood there, handsome and grinning.

The harper said, "Boy, go after that dog."

The boy leapt for that thread. He shinned up it as fast as any other boy ever shinned up a ladder. He too vanished.

Again the bard turned to his bag. This time too he had trouble, but before long a young woman stood there, so beautiful that every man caught his breath and forgot all about the wonders in the clouds.

"Girl, go after the others," the stranger told her, "and see to it that the hound does not tear the hare. That boy may be careless."

She went, and a groaning "Ah-h" rose from the throats of all the young men. They would have liked her to stay where they could get at her.

But she too vanished, and soon, mixed with the sound of the hound's belling that still came down to them from the sky, sweet and wild and strange, came the two young people's voices calling to him. All of Caswallon's people, and all of Pryderi's, stood there in awe, listening to that hunt in the sky, until at last all the lovely, strange sound of it died away. Then silence fell; an awed, stunned silence.

Until the bard shook his head and frowned. "I am afraid," said he, looking up into the clouds, "that there are goings-on up there."

"What kind of goings-on?" asked Caswallon.

"I am afraid that the hound is eating up the hare, while the boy makes love to the girl."

All the young fellows there stiffened or snorted. One said angrily, "A bad servant that fellow is, letting his master down like that. I would have the hide off him for that!"

But really each was angry only because it was not himself who was doing that lovemaking. Each thought enviously what a soft bed that white cloud must make, only Pryderi remembered red-haired Kigva waiting for him at home, and grinned in sympathy.

Caswallon's stern mouth twitched. "That is likely enough," he said.

"Well, I will put a stop to it," said the stranger. And he took out the ball again and began to reel the thread in. Once more all eyes were glued to that gleaming roundness . . .

Then all of a sudden both girl and boy were sprawling on the ground together, and nobody at all could have had any doubt as to what they had been doing. Next instant the dog plopped down beside them, one of the hare's legs still sticking out of his mouth.

Everybody there roared with laughter, even Caswallon. Everybody but the bard. His jaw set and he drew his sword and advanced upon the lovers. In one flash the boy's head was off his shoulders and spinning along the ground. The body twitched like a beheaded chicken's.

Men gasped. Women screamed. Caswallon sobered and his eyes pinned the stranger's. "I do not like a thing of that sort to be done before me," he said with dignity.

A man near the house wall muttered, "Unless he does it himself." And then wished he had been silent, for in that sudden deep silence even whispers were loud.

The stranger shrugged. "Well, Lord King, if you are not pleased, what has been done can be undone."

Pryderi sank back into his chair and drew a long breath of relief. Until then he had not known how shocked and somehow disappointed he was. Inexplicably, since this manslayer was only a chance-met stranger.

"Undo it then," said Caswallon harshly.

The harper walked over to the head and picked it up. He threw it toward the still twitching body and it lit on the neck and promptly grew fast there. The boy sprang up, looking startled. But soon he looked more startled, for his face was looking out over his back, not over his chest. His head had been put on the wrong way round.

"Better for him to die than to live like that!" said Caswallon violently.

"I am glad you think so," said the stranger. He went up to the boy then and put a hand on either side of his face. Without effort he twisted the head around until it faced the right way again.

"Get back into the bag now," he said. "The lot of you."

They shrank and dwindled; the lovers became the size of children, the dog became the size of a pup, and the meat jumped out of its mouth and became a whole hare again, though a tiny one. They all ran for the bag and by the time they reached it they were the size of dolls. They scrambled into it and were gone.

The stranger picked up his bag and his harp and started for the gate. But Caswallon's voice leapt after him like a spear. "Stop that man!"

Men raced forward, massed themselves before the gates, the sunlight gleaming on their spearpoints.

The bard stopped. Unhurried, the King walked up to him. "So it is war, Manawyddan my cousin?"

No muscle of the other's face changed. "It is peace if you will have it, Caswallon."

The High King laughed. "That is not for you to

offer. Not with my men between you and the gate. I do not think that you can climb over them on that thread of yours."

He saw the memory that Manawyddan did not try to hide, and laughed. "It takes time to weave invisibility for oneself. Time such as I had when I prepared my attack upon the Seven who guarded Caradoc. I will not give it to you."

The son of Llyr said, unmoved, "Trick for trick, magic for magic, I can match you, Caswallon. And master you. Did you forget, because Bran and I seldom chose to play such children's games, that we were of the Old Blood, and knew more of Illusion and Fantasy than you could ever hope to learn?"

"I do not deny it. But men bar the gates against you now, cousin. Sharp spears end all Illusions."

Pryderi came up to them then, his eyes dangerous, his young mouth set. "This man came here in my following, Lord; so he is under my protection. What has he done that you should slay him?"

Manawyddan spoke before Caswallon could. "None seeks to slay me, young Lord. The High King and I have matters of which we must talk alone."

And Pryderi, to his own surprise, turned and went back to his seat.

Manawyddan said quietly to Caswallon, "He does not know who I am. Such glamor is on his eyes as still rests upon all here save yours. For awhile I blinded those too."

"Not for long. You came here to guard your whelp—though you hoped to find a chance to take my life at the same time."

"I did come to guard the boy; that much truth even you can still see, cousin. But whether he dies now or in old age he never will doubt that he is the son of Pwyll, Prince of Dyved. Crowns and thrones are toys I never would shed blood for— least of all would I ever risk his blood for them."

"You say that, but how can I trust you? You have caught me in a trap, Manawyddan, but it is you and your son who will die in it. Black as my name will be, I will still be King. A man can bear the burdens he must."

Manawyddan laughed. "My Illusion is upon your men's eyes; you know that. If I turn now and cry, 'Here I come!' each will see my face upon the head of the man next to him. While they are killing each other, Pryderi and I and all who follow him can go out by other doors."

Caswallon said grimly, "If that is so, why do you not make them see your face on my face, and make an end?"

"Because then I must sit where now you sit, and as uncomfortably. For we both have friends. I myself cannot see why it matters whether a man's own son succeeds him or his sister's son, so long as the new king serves the people well."

Caswallon's lip curled. "You give yourself one more reason to seek my place, father of Pryderi."

"It is your place, so long as you use it well. I do not say that I will make no move if you oppress the people, but I am still the fool you have always thought me. I would hate to make that move. For then I too would have blood on my hands, I too would always be looking back over my shoulder. I do not want that burden, nor will I put it upon Pryderi, whose nature is not fitted to bear it."

Caswallon said slowly, "The burden is heavy. But I do not hate it enough to lay it down. You must know that you can never trust me, cousin. Are you fool enough to let me live, knowing that?"

"I can trust you, cousin. Because I have too much knowledge for you ever to be able to creep upon me unsuspected, under any Veil of Illusion. And you know now that I can always creep upon you unseen. I will go now, and you will keep faith with Pryderi, knowing that I have power to avenge him. Also, when your men come to take the Holy Stones, your High Druid will come with them, to tell all men that Pryderi bowed to the Gods' own will.

"Fare as well as you can, cousin. As boys we two played better games than today's together, but I hope that in these bodies we now wear we will never meet again."

Caswallon bit his lip, then signed to his guards. As mist melts before the summer sun, so they melted away from the gate. Without a backward look the stranger who was Manawyddan son of Llyr turned his back upon them and strode out.

"He might have said goodbye at least," one of Pryderi's men grumbled.

But Pryderi was staring after him in wonder. He said slowly, "I know him now. I should have known him when first I saw him. He is the harper who came to Teyrnon's house in Gwent long ago, when I was little."

7

The Taking of the Holy Stones

Again Pryderi, the son of Pwyll, came home to Arberth, and again his people welcomed him. Torches burned like stars, and roasting beasts and birds smoked over gleaming fires, and harpers played and told their tales. But Pryderi bore with all that only to keep from hurting his people's feelings.

"I have had too much feasting and too much drinking and too much merrymaking," he told his family, when he was alone with them. "I need some fresh air. The Gods know how I need it after sitting all those nights with Caswallon's smile on me."

"You said the King received you well, Son." Rhiannon smiled her own gentle yet somehow mocking smile.

"He did so, but I do not like that smile of his. It is full of teeth and full of smugness and full of whiskers. It makes you feel as if he were a cat that had just swallowed a mouse, and you are not sure that you are not the mouse. Indeed—" and he sobered, "it was wiped off his face once, though. And that was a strange happening."

He told them then of the mysterious harper, and of how at last he had known him for the same man who had played before Teyrnon in Gwent, long ago.

"He did you great good then, Mother. Can it be that not all your kinsmen in the Bright World are so set against you after all?"

"None of them are set against me, Son. It is I that cut myself off from them, leaving the world of my birth to follow your father."

"So you always say. But then who put those years of barrenness on you? And who had me carried off on my birth night, when I finally got myself born at last?"

Rhiannon's smile deepened. "You take too much credit to yourself, Son. Your father and I were the ones who got you born."

"That is not the point. You know what I mean . . ."

But Kigva was bubbling over with wonder. "By the Mothers! How I wish I could see that strange man and thank him! Except for him you might never have come home to us. For why did he appear again unless Caswallon was plotting something against you?"

"That is true." Pryderi sobered again. "I have been wondering about that myself."

Manawyddan said, "Arawn, King of Annwn, owes your father much, lad. His whole Otherworldly kingdom. Maybe he wished Caswallon to know that you had strong friends."

Rhiannon said gravely, "There are many worlds, most of them better than this, a few worse. We who live in this one cannot know any ways but its ways. Even I cannot, many of whose memories went from me when my flesh coarsened into earthly flesh. Let us waste no time in vain wonderings. You are home again, Son; that is enough."

"It is indeed!" Kigva caught his hand and squeezed it. "But—" her eyes widened, "what if that Caswallon visits us here sometime? I do not want to sleep with him!"

Rhiannon laughed softly. "You will not have to, child. That night I will put your shape on a cow or a mare. Or a she-rat if I can catch one. She should make Caswallon a proper bedmate; true flesh of his flesh."

Pryderi and Kigva laughed heartily, but both looked relieved. Pryderi said, "But what about my fresh air? It seems to me that everybody in Dyved wants to sit here and eat until next year."

"Tell them you, who have been away so long, wish to make the circuit of your dominions," said Rhiannon. "Indeed, it is high time you did just that. Then every chief and rich farmer will go home and make his house and folk fine for you."

"And a good thing that will be too," she told Manawyddan later, when they were in bed. "For though our many guests have brought many gifts, the palace stores are getting low. When we ourselves are the guests and our hosts have to furnish all the food the feasts will not last so long."

Manawyddan laughed and hugged her. "You are a good housewife, Lady. You have learned the ways of our world well. Yet sometimes I wonder— can it be that you never regret your own?"

"Lord, I rode after Pwyll into the teeth of time, that I knew must tear us and gut us and fling us away like gnawed bones at last. I will not say I came without dread, but I came by my own choice."

"It was a great and unheard-of choice."

"It was. Yet all seems like a dream now, that Land of the Ever-Young, where people never die until they grow too wise for our world, and so ready for the next—one that we know as little of as you do of ours."

"So I have heard. And that death among you is different from our death."

"It is only deep sleep, without illness. Well I remember my fear when I first saw the ugliness of earthly death, and knew that it must come to me, and might come first to him—to Pwyll. But not even then did I regret.

"I have sorrowed, but I have not been sorry for my choice. And here tonight I am not sorry, Manawyddan, son of Llyr." Once more she put her arms about his neck . . .

So began for Manawyddan the happiness in Dyved, those long good days in that land that poets later were to call the Land of Magic and Illusion. He and Rhiannon rode with Pryderi and Kigva through those green fields, and thought that they never had seen crops richer than those crops, tasted honey sweeter than that honey. To Pryderi it was home, the home that he had long been away from. And to Kigva any land through which she rode with him would have seemed as sweet as Rhiannon's lovely Land of the Ever-Young. The glamour that was upon their young eyes gilded the eyes of the older couple also; they thought that they never before had realized the goodness and the magical simplicity of earth.

The *Mabinogi* says that those four were happy together; that they became such friends that they could not bear to be parted by day or by night. That sounds unlikely; each couple must have wanted some privacy; but surely they were happy.

They lacked nothing but the son Pryderi had wanted. He would have been very welcome, but he was not really needed. For they had enough, and rarely indeed can human beings claim that most perfect of conditions, they who live oftenest in hope of the future, and then, when that piece of it that they have planned and labored for comes, must live on and work on in the hope of a new piece.

Having enough—that hardest of all sums to obtain and the most impossible to keep—those four were very delicately poised upon a wonderful and slippery height. Their perfect balance, their deep content, could not last long; for it is the nature of time both to add and to take away.

Manawyddan and Rhiannon must have known that, and have talked of it.

She said, "For long I feared time, Lord, I who knew that it must take away my lover's strength and my beauty. But after Pwyll died I learned to bless it because now it had done its worst and could only bring me nearer to him."

"I understand," said Manawyddan. And sighed, thinking of Bran and Branwen.

"But when I had blessed it my vision changed, I saw that it was a teacher as well as a destroyer. I saw that, great as was my love and Pwyll's, I must not make a prison of its memory, a walled place, shutting others out. For every walled place is truly a small place, cramping the body and the spirit. And every man and woman is worthy of love, and each calls forth a love that can be given only to himself or herself, never to another. And I remembered you, and knew that I loved you, and that by that loving I need not cease to love Pwyll. It is hard to make clear, that lesson. Do you understand, Lord?"

Manawyddan said, "I do."

She shivered slightly. "Change will come again, I know—change the child of time. And I fear Caswallon your cousin. Do you really think that he can take away the Holy Stones?"

"I think so. He is sure of it, and in matters that deal with matter my cousin is no fool."

"Would to the Mothers that you could have kept him from tricking that promise out of Pryderi! Nothing could put such fear on the folk of Dyved as the going of the Stones. And it will be a weapon in the hands of the chiefs of the Seven Cantrevs of Seissyllwch too. They do not love Pryderi."

Manawyddan frowned. "I know. Those Seven Cantrevs were part of Dyved until the New Tribes came, and then, in Bran's last year, because the chiefs who held them were misusing the Old Tribesmen still there—as Pwyll never used those under him—my brother gave Pryderi leave to break the peace and to take back those Seven Cantrevs. And the poor folk in them have cause to bless your son, but those chiefs will always curse him."

"Yes." She shivered again. "I am not likely to forget that war, Lord. It was Pryderi's first, and he rode to it laughing. But I wondered if I ever would laugh again in this body. If he had died like his father . . . !"

His hand covered hers. "In the end you would have blessed time again, Lady, but it would have been hard."

"Too hard!" She clutched at him and her body shook. "That would have been the one thing I could not have borne. No man ever can quite understand the bond between a woman and the child that is born of her body—not even you, Manawyddan, wisest of men!"

"Something of that too I know, my Rhiannon." His voice was deep, heavy with unsayable things. He held her, he spoke her name, but he saw, not her face but Branwen's face, as it had looked on that black night outside Tara, when she had seen her little son thrown into the fire by Evnissyen, their hate-crazed brother; Evnissyen, who should never have been born.

Rhiannon heard and saw, she thought that his pain was for what might have befallen Pryderi. She said quickly, "Well I know that you love him too, Lord! You have guarded him and watched over him as well as any father could. But it is not the same."

He could not tell even her of Branwen, of that old pain. He thought, *This is excess, and therefore dangerous. Any lover has a right to die to save the beloved. As I would have died for Branwen, or Bran, or Nissyen. Or for Branwen's baby. But to lay all life waste because of what cannot be saved—that is to yield yourself up to the Destroyer you hate. To set your will against the will of the Mothers. But who am I to tell a woman how to serve the Mothers?*

Least of all this woman who had reawakened in him the joy of life . . .

He said aloud, "Lady, many of the druids Caswallon has talked with are wise men, though he is not. And my heart tells me that it is right for the Stones to go; that in their new home they will be a wonder and a mystery to men through the ages. As for Pryderi, we have given him life; from now on all we can do for him is to give him what love and counsel he is willing to accept from us."

His lady smiled tolerantly and tenderly upon him. She thought, *So the wisest of men is as foolish as the rest, after all.*

They went on being happy. Earth was their mother and their friend; for life itself is magical and the Great Energy that shapes all things a magician mightier than any Man of Illusion and Fantasy that the Welsh ever knew. The miracles we see daily seem commonplace and what the Head of Bran did at Gwales wonderful, only because the one event is seldom heard of, and the others happen all the time. Yet a Head that talks after being cut from its shoulders is not, if we stop to think, nearly so vast or all-moving a Mystery as the wonders of growth, or of sunrise and sunset.

We have made of "natural" and "everyday" poor words, ordinary and trite, when they should be *the* Word, full of awesome magic and might; of cosmic power.

On Gwales, Manawyddan had been less awake

than he was in Dyved. Or perhaps more awake, because there he had lived in eternity, and outside time. He had forgotten that Bran was dead, because Bran was there. Now he was caught again in the ancient inexorable pattern of time and loss, but again his feet were set upon a road, and the new pattern was weaving round him, rich in color and music. Rhiannon wove it, Rhiannon with her deep eyes and her warm mouth and her understanding that usually was as full and sweet and quiet as her breast. She was like cool water on sun-baked earth; like a warm fire in the chill of an autumn night.

"Best to love in the afternoon," he told her once. "After the storm, when the heart has learned wisdom and the body is not yet too old. When love is no longer strain and fear and wine that goes to a man's head, but the fire on his hearth and the food on his table."

She smiled her twisted smile, half elf's, half mother's. "Pryderi and Kigva would think that spent old man's talk. They are eating each other like honey. Am I no more to you now than a well-burning faggot or a well-done joint of beef? Time was when I could make a man drunk."

His eyes danced. "Let us see what you can do now. It is not spent I feel yet, Lady."

And presently she said that he was not, indeed . . .

Winter laid whiteness upon the hillsides. The winds shrieked and howled; they raged through that ancient Ring of the Holy Stones, as if striving to overturn what had stood before any green thing grew on earth; before life first took on a shape that breathed and moved. Cold as ice those winds blew; like knives they pierced all living flesh. But in the great hall at Arberth there was fire and warmth and laughter; summer still bloomed.

Spring came, and with it the men of Caswallon. Unarmed they came, save for sledges of heavy wood and ropes of twisted hides. They broke up the Ring, they moved the Holy Stones, those firstborn of Earth the Mother. In Her flesh they left torn holes, where of old Her children had stood.

The people of Dyved cried out in horror. They left their ploughs in the field, their food half-eaten on the table. They rushed to arms, but Pryderi had to stop them; to say, "I have promised . . ."

The High Druid spoke; he whom Caswallon had sent, as Manawyddan had bidden him. He said that this was the Will of the Gods, revealed to him himself, as he slept before the altar, upon a bull's hide. How the Holy Stones, the Unmoving First Folk, were going now to a place where they would be seen and honored by more folk than ever before. By the whole Island of the Mighty.

In silence the people of Dyved listened. Their faces did not lighten; they only lost what light the fire of battle had given them. In bewilderment and woe they watched that unarmed host drag the Stones away.

Some muttered, "They cannot get far. Their backs will break from weariness. They will slink away, back to this thieving High King, like hounds whipped away from the kill. And we will go to the Folk That Do Not Move, and bring them home again."

But others said despairingly, "The High Druid dreamed it. Upon the bull's hide he dreamed."

A few said, "Never would Pwyll have let the Stones go. If he had been alive . . ."

Yet fewer said, "If only he had married a woman of his own people, begotten a son who cared for his own folk . . ."

Bent beneath that load that seemed more than men could bear, Caswallon's men toiled toward the sea. Long and hard was that toil; their arms were almost torn from their sockets, their backs seemed bowed forever, but at last they came to the gray billowing water, to the waiting rafts. By sea the Stones fared then until they reached the mouth of a river deep enough to float them. From stream to stream they passed; long and winding as a snake was that road. But at last they came to their appointed place; in the midst of greenness, within a ring of giant sarsen stones, their own Ring was set up again. The Holy Place stood, and stands yet, and still men marvel.

Later men were to say that only magic could have moved those Stones; that wise Merlin, Arthur's guardian, brought them from Ireland. And indeed it may be that the New Tribes, or some part of them, had come into Dyved from Ireland.

But the only magic that moved those Stones was Caswallon's shrewd and ruthless will. He planned well.

In Dyved people still muttered, "Evil will come. Our luck has gone with the First Folk."

Summer wore. Their crops grew tall and golden, but still they stared at the sky, in dread of storm. All who could shunned the hills, but those who could not walked warily, each looking upward or westward or downward; anywhere but toward the spot that each man still saw stark and clear before him. That empty place upon the windy heights where from times unremembered the Stones had stood, guarding Dyved. Where they stood no longer, those Holy Ones, the first born of the Mother.

8

Storm over the Gorsedd Arberth

The rains ceased; the heat grew; the sun burned down upon the broad brown breast of the Mother, as if hating Her and all the life that sprang from Her. The fear in the folk's eyes changed. Some said, "We did wrong to fear the storm." And others added, "It is this way that the doom is to come."

Rhiannon said, "There may be something that I can do about this." And she called her women together, and all the other women that would follow her, and led them to a place deep in the woods. There they waited until the moon rose and what rites they performed then no man ever knew. Only shepherds and goatherds heard their singing, faint and far off, and loved the sound, yet shivered at it.

Dawn came, but quietly, without her wonted blaze of gold. Clouds veiled the sun's fierce face; the darkness gave way only to grayness, not to true light. And soon rain began to fall; like a myriad soft tiny paws it pattered upon the parched earth, upon the dying things that had been green.

It saved the crops. And then it stopped.

The sun shone upon the reapers. Men and women sang as they gathered in the harvest. Most said, "The old Queen is wise and mighty. She has appeased the wrath of the Gods." But some still said, "Wait."

In the great hall at Arberth a feast was spread. Men drank in celebration, drank to their own strength, and to Earth the fruitful Mother, to her who, with the help of that strength, had brought forth. For now they were sure of another winter's food, and food is life. All eyes turned with love to Pryderi; the harvest is good only when the King is good. He had not failed them; his power and luck were still with him, even though he had let himself—and them—be tricked out of the Holy Stones.

Pryderi knew what was in their hearts. For moons that knowledge had burned him, and the saving rain had not altogether eased that burning. For he knew that he had had no hand in bringing it.

He was too honest to forget that, and he was too young not to need to prove himself to himself. *Since I have not done this, this thing for which I am praised, I must do something as good. As worthy of praise.*

He rose, cup in hand. He said, "Drink this drink with me, men and women of Dyved. For by sun and moon, by earth and air, I swear that I will not eat or drink again until I have watched the sun rise from the Gorsedd Arberth."

There was silence then. Eye sought eye, and each was a terror and a question. Even by day, when the sun was high, men shunned the mighty Mound called the Gorsedd Arberth. By night even they who lived in the palace below it walked as far from it as they could, and shuddered when they heard a night bird call from its lonely heights. It was a place of power; of too much power for man.

Manawyddan looked at Rhiannon, and saw her face calm and still, masklike as the moon's. But her hands were tightly clenched; so tightly that the piece of bread in one of them was crumbling. And Kigva's round young face was white with fear.

Again Pryderi spoke, his voice loud and clear, so that all might hear. "Few Princes of Dyved have done this deed, but each Prince has known that he must stand ready to do it. Pwyll my father did it after he came back from Annwn; he who had walked in the Land of the Dead knew that he must cleanse himself of the death that still clung to him and win new power and life from the Mighty Ones of the Mound—including a Queen to bear his sons—or else go down again into the Underworld forever. And the Mound-Dwellers honored him above all men by sending him one of their own—the Lady, my mother." He paused and smiled at her, then faced the folk again.

"Now I, who have been farther away from my people than any Prince but Pwyll ever was, will dare the same adventure. I will prove once and for all that no ill luck is on me—that no doom has followed me home from that terrible great war beyond the sea. I will take what the Gods send me!"

He drained the cup, laughed, and flung it from him, the smile on his young face bright as flame. As one man, his people rose, shouted and cheered him. All the young men shouted, "We will go with you!"

He smiled. "It is your right. My father went with his foster-brothers round him, and all his true companions."

Kigva rose, the daughter of Gwynn Gloyu, and the girlishness was gone from her young face; it was a woman's. "It is my right also, Pryderi. Of old, Queens mounted the Mount to die with their Kings."

"Or to be wedded to them anew." Manawyddan rose. "There is no need for dying now. But when you went into battle overseas, stepson, we two always went side by side."

Pryderi said in dismay, "I thought to leave the Queens in your care, second-father. Kigva has nothing to prove; let her wait here in our chamber, to hold the Holy Marriage with me when I return."

Rhiannon rose and threw her bread to a hound. "Kigva has already claimed her right, Son. And I stood upon the Gorsedd before you were born. I do not fear to stand there tonight."

In the end they all went, even the ladies who waited on Rhiannon and Kigva.

They bore no torches. The moon was full, and the top of the Gorsedd would be light as day. But though the way was short, part of it lay through the deep shadow of the Mound, and in that blackness none could see another's face. They could hear only footsteps, small scrunching sounds that seemed to disturb both the pebbled earth and her silence. Each heard his or her own breathing, too, and that seemed loud, another affront to that deep shroud of silence. Many thought wistfully of the torchlit hall where, but a little while before, they had been so merry. Where now the servants were eating the broken food left by the great ones— could it really be only a few paces away?

Will we ever get back there? Ever laugh and drink again? That mute cry rose from a hundred hearts.

In the darkness Rhiannon's hand slipped into Manawyddan's.

He said, "Fear nothing, my Queen. Had the harvest not been good these 'true companions' might have seen signs bidding them slay him, but not now. He has won back their love."

She laughed shortly. "The last Prince who mounted the Gorsedd before Pwyll died—beaten to death with his own men's spears, I think. But that is not what I fear. Here on this Mound there is indeed a door into another world—that I know well, who once came through it."

Manawyddan was silent, thinking of what else might have come through it. Of that huge grisly Arm that had taken her newborn son from her side.

Rhiannon said, "There was no need for this. Before the rain came I feared that he might have to do it. But now, when all was well! What got into him? If it is some spell that is on him, drawing him to doom—" She shuddered.

Manawyddan said, "It is only himself. His pride has been hurt. Also I think he truly fears that the ill luck that came on us in Ireland clouded his judgment and so made him lose the Stones."

"And that too was only himself! His prudence

has always been the least part of him. It is a pity that children's heads do not grow up as fast as the rest of them. Now I must watch him running into danger that once I could have pulled him back from—by the ear, if need be!"

"Lady, that last is the fate of all parents who see a child live to grow up."

"I know, but that does not make it less hard! If only I could have taught him more! But when I came through those doors that now I can re-enter only by dying your earth-death, I forgot much— and on much that I do remember my lips are sealed."

They went on in silence.

They came out of that depth of shadow, and found themselves at the foot of the Mound, their people about them. Ahead of them Pryderi and Kigva were already climbing, hand in hand, the girl bright-faced again because of that clasp. The elder couple followed, and the moon looked down on them with her pale, battered stare, like a golden face mauled by fiends from outer space.

They came to the top of the Mound. They sat down together, the four of them, upon the stones that had been set there, how long ago no man remembered, to serve as seats at such times as these. They sat there, with their train of folk around them.

They sat and waited . . .

They saw light below them, streaming out of the open doors of the palace they had left. Faintly voices seemed to be borne to them.

Kigva said, low, "I thought our housefolk liked us. How can they be so glad?"

Rhiannon said, "They do, but now the wine is in them, and drowns all else. And maybe not only wine. Do not begrudge them their moment of being masters and mistresses of all they work for every day, but never own."

And indeed, all of them there on that dreaded height felt like the dead looking back into the world of the living. Into a space and a life already far away, incredibly remote. Silence seemed to be wrapping around them, fold after fold of it, an ever-thickening cloak. It got into their mouths and into their minds; it stole over them like sleep.

Then from far off, faintly, sweetly, came the sound of music. Music more beautiful than the song of birds, gentler than the lowest note of the lullaby in the throat of a mother who lulls her child to sleep.

Manawyddan felt peace coming over him and his lids closing, and then suddenly he felt something else—a sharp, jabbing pain. He started awake, reaching for his sword. But he saw no monster, but only his lady's white fingers leaving his arm, and then a yelp told him that she had also pinched her son.

"Ouch!" Pryderi rubbed himself. "It is my opinion, Mother, that there has been nothing dangerous here on the Gorsedd since you came out of it!"

But Rhiannon did not seem to hear him. She was looking into the vast dark sky, as if it were a face, and hers was whiter than the moon could ever make it. She was muttering, charms and words of power, but the deep strong sound of them, in some tongue that was soft as the rustling of leaves; a tongue not of earth. Both men knew that much; their hair rose on their heads as if given legs by the strangeness of the sound, and Kigva clung to a hand of each.

She too was awake, but no other man or woman on that hill was. All their heads were bowed, all their bodies slumped or sprawled, in deepest sleep. Like tall plants mown down by a scythe they lay there, or drooped in their places, emptied and soulless as dead folk yet unburied.

Rhiannon's muttering ceased. She turned and faced the three, and sweat stood like dew upon her brow.

"You fools! Would you sleep upon the Mound of Arberth? Better to sleep in the middle of the sea with no boat beneath you, or in the fireplace with the fire lit!"

They tried to answer her, they opened their mouths, but nothing came out. Their jaws only widened in great yawns. The night was still again; clouds gathered round the moon like sheep huddling round their shepherd.

Or like wolves closing in upon a sheep . . .

Manawyddan thought in angry surprise, *My mind is awake, but my body is not.* He braced himself and began to fight.

His lids felt heavy; very heavy; never in his life had he tried to hold up anything so heavy. He saw that Pryderi's eyes had already closed again, and that Kigva's were closing.

Rhiannon swayed, looking from one dulled face to another. Both her lips and her fingers worked, as if she did not know which to use first.

Then Manawyddan's eyes flashed open. He shook Pryderi awake, and Rhiannon did the same

for Kigva. He drew his own sword and then Pryderi's, and thrust the blade into the younger man's
slack hand.

"We must walk. Round and round, sunwise.
And if one tries to fall out of the circle, the one
behind must prick or pinch him!"

They did so. They stumbled, their eyes kept
closing; it was as if stones were tied to their legs,
dragging them down. But they kept moving; their
circle was not broken.

Rhiannon's tired eyes began to shine. She whispered to Manawyddan, "If we can only hold out
till sunrise . . ."

Silence fell again. They stumbled on, their eyes
clinging desperately, hopefully, to the still black-
ened east.

The moon was gone; the clouds had swallowed
her. There was no light anywhere; only darkness
and that deep silence.

Suddenly Kigva looked around her and behind
her, like a child that is afraid. She said, "It is too
still. It is as if the earth too were frightened and
waiting for something to happen. I would like to
hear a noise; any noise in the world."

Like an answer, thunder crashed around them;
like a hammer big as the biggest mountain it
smote the earth. All caught at their ears with the
pain of it; they felt as if their eardrums had been
smashed and had fallen back bleeding into their
skulls.

Like a sea, mist fell from heaven. They saw it
boiling white above their heads, between them
and the black sky; thick as sea water, furious as
foam, falling, falling.

Then it was upon them, around them, and they were each alone in a terrible roaring world that had neither color nor form left in it, not even the negative color of darkness.

They could not see each other. They could not see anything. They knew that the earth was yet beneath their feet but only because they felt it there.

Manawyddan felt as if he were fighting to keep his head from being blown away, from rocking, away like a bobbing ball upon that immense stream of sound, that incredible and unheard-of din; the roar of that storm that was like no storm of earth.

He groped, like a blind man, with his hands. "Rhiannon! Pryderi! Kigva! Give me your hands! We must keep our circle. We must not let one another go!"

Several times he had to shout that, each time louder, before he could hear his own voice. Then at last he felt Pryderi's strong palm slip into his, and on the other side of him Rhiannon's smooth one; and he heard her voice, that carried through the wind and the thunder like the thin clear ring of a silver bell. "I have one of Kigva's hands. Have either of you men got the other?"

Pryderi tried to say yes, but the rushing sound carried away his voice.

They stood with clasped hands, those four; the thunder cudgeled their ears; the wind lashed them like an icy flail acres long, acres wide. Kigva was knocked to her knees. Manawyddan said, "Better if we all lie down. But we must not let go each other's hands."

They lay there, hands still tightly clasped. The wind could no longer beat them, but they shivered in its icy, unnatural cold. It roared through the vault of night like the waves of a roaring sea, an ocean risen out of its immemorial gulf to drown all life. Again and again the thunder crashed; it seemed that the Mound itself must be leveled, and earth herself break apart and fall into the vast abyss of outer space.

Yet even through that din they began to distinguish other sounds; tiny, far off, they rose from below. Thin and feeble as the piping of insects, they yet pierced that mightiness of sound, and with a terrible finality. Shrieks, the death cries of men and beasts.

The four shuddered; they clasped one another's hands yet more tightly, hearing their world die.

But all things end except ourselves, and even those, as we know them, have an end . . .

They did not know when the roar slackened. They were too deafened to think; the noise had got into their heads and rolled on there, dazing and ceaseless.

But they saw the mist begin to thin. When they began to see one another as dim blobs thicker than the surrounding dimness, their stunned minds woke. Anxiously they watched those blobs take on shape, line; saw those blurred forms sprout faces, become individuals again.

There is something left. We are here; we have each other. The world goes on.

Morning was coming; the mist was almost shining now. Through it Pryderi's hair gleamed golden. Kigva's red hair lit itself again like a torch.

Manwyddan's eyes found Rhiannon's, and they smiled at each other.

The sun came up red, proudly, reclaiming her own. The whole sky glowed with a light that was pure and pale as pearl. Defeated, the mist shrank down through that new gentle silence, to the earth below.

The four looked around them, and saw that on that bare hilltop they were alone.

Not one of all those who had followed them up that hill was there. They had vanished, as if dissolved in the mist.

Kigva caught Pryderi's hand. "Did the wind blow them away?"

He said, through stiff lips, "I do not know."

All four looked down; intently, desperately, as if their eyes were spears or arrows that could pierce that white blanket of mist that still lay below.

It, too, was thinning. Soon the thatched roofs of the palace began to rise through it, the roofs of home, and for a breath's space the sight was sweeter than honey, like a mother's face to a lost child. Then, "There should be smoke coming up," cried Manawyddan. "There is none."

"Maybe the wind blew all the fires out," said Pryderi. "Let us go down and see."

He started down, but Rhiannon caught his arm. "Wait, Son. Let us see a little more."

They waited, they watched. Soon they could see the good everyday green and brown of earth. But something was wrong, something was different. They strained their eyes, peering down into countryside that should have been filled with peaceful farms; with the fields and herds and the small snug dwellings of folks.

It was not. Only the fields were left, the quiet, empty fields. The trees and the green meadows.

There was no house, no beast, no man. Not even any charred ruin where lightning-blasted houses might have stood.

Terror clutched their hearts like iron fingers. They ran stumbling down the hillside. They came to the palace. Its doors were not barred and bolted against the storm. They stood wide open, black mouths of desolation.

They went inside, and no man greeted them. The great hall stood empty, except for overthrown chairs and tables, and dishes and spilled food littering the floor.

They searched the whole palace, the sleeping-places, the storehouses and the kitchens, and still found nothing but food and furniture and garments, all tossed and broken and torn by that mighty wind. No living thing was left, not even a dog.

They cried into that silence, that was no longer menacing, but only empty. That gave them back nothing but the echo of their own voices.

Pryderi stopped at last and scratched his head. "Everybody in Dyved must have been blown away," he said.

Kigva clung to him, her teeth chattering. "What does it mean? What does it all mean?"

Sudden hope lit his eyes. "Maybe we are dreaming," he said. And he pinched her arm experimentally.

"Ouch!" said Kigva. "You need not do that to

see if I am real. I will see if you are." And she pinched him.

"Indeed," said Pryderi, "there are pleasanter ways of proving it."

He gave her a kiss on the mouth then, and she gave that back to him also. They kissed each other several times, and began to look as if they felt better. Rhiannon looked at them soberly.

"You should not have challenged my people, Son. When a man stands upon the Gorsedd Arberth, he takes his mind along with him, and they can seize that mind, and use it. When I was of that world and longed for your father Pwyll, I could not come to him until he sat upon that Mound and so placed himself and his own world within my reach."

Manawyddan said, "We had better eat and sleep now. Then we can go forth and see if the whole land is like this."

For a day and a night they rested, and then they set out. They searched from end to end of Dyved, but they found neither man, woman, nor child. Neither cattle nor sheep, nor even a lost dog. Man, and every living thing that belonged to man, had been swept away.

Nearer the sea they did find empty houses. White butterflies flew strangely thick around these, and sometimes one would fly into a vacant house and touch some object—bowl or bed or garment—tenderly and lingeringly with their delicate minute feelers, as if it were something that they loved.

Manawyddan and Rhiannon looked sadly at

each other when they saw those little winged visitors.

"It is such shapes that the lesser druids claim to see come forth from the mouths of the dying," he said. "Are all our people dead then? We have found no bodies or bones."

Rhiannon shook her head. "Hard it is to tell what has happened. We do not know what glamour may yet be over our own eyes. But I am sure that our people have died no ordinary death. Maybe they were too afraid, and all of them that was gross matter shook to pieces under the force of His will that sent this Illusion forth. For it is an Illusion that has come on Dyved—a spell from my own world, and so is Gwawl avenged at last."

"You think that the Avenger was one, not many?"

Her eyes half closed. "I do not know. I cannot say. It took great power."

"Well, what matters is this—will what has been done content the doer? Or the doers?"

She shivered as if a cold wind had touched her. As if the inner light of her flickered in some unearthly chill.

"Again I do not know. I cannot be sure—they tried hard to take us that night. I used all the power I had left, and when that was gone you saved us. They may be satisfied, seeing us brought down from kings and queens to wanderers in a waste."

"It is not a bad life this is," said Manawyddan. "We have our health and ourselves, and the sky is blue above us, and the sun shines on us. If now we have to hunt and fish to feed ourselves, yet the lands we live and work in are our own, and the food when we get it the sweeter-flavored for being a greater prize."

"That is so," said Rhiannon. "And a good reason why they may not be willing to leave us in peace."

9

The Change

Autumn came like a torch, and set the trees on fire. The birds flew away to warmer lands, but still Manawyddan and Pryderi hunted and fished, and Rhiannon and Kigva cooked what they brought home. Winter came, and white snow, and again winds howled over Dyved, though not such winds as had howled on that terrible night. The men sat at home oftener, and Rhiannon and Kigva made bread from the crops that had been harvested before the Terror came.

Spring came again, and greenness, and birds. And again they left the palace, those four, and went wandering through the land, living on game and wild honey. Until autumn came again, and another winter.

No man came near them. No travelers or messengers entered Dyved, and at first that seemed strange. But Manawyddan said, "The druids must have seen in their crystals something of what befell on that night of doom. They think us gone with the others, and strangers fear to enter and take possession lest the curse still cling to the land and rise and smite them." He did not add, No doubt they think that no curse would have come had the Holy Stones stayed at home in their ancient places.

Pryderi snorted. "Caswallon must be pleased. He thinks he is rid of you for good."

"So he is," said Manawyddan. "Certainly we four never will go up against him in battle. Doubtless he would make us welcome if we came to his court seeking his bounty—then he could show all men our poverty and his kindliness. But that too I think we would not wish to do."

Pryderi snorted again. "It is the last thing we would do! And I think it would be the last, for I would hate to trust my head long to that kindliness of his. The very thought makes it feel loose on my shoulders."

"You wrong him there," said Manawyddan. "None could be more tender of our lives. He would, as I have said, make a great show of us."

"We could go to Mâth, the Ancient in Gwynedd," said Kigva. "He might be able to help us. No man on earth is said to be mightier in Illusion and Fantasy than He."

"No power on earth could match the Power that has struck down Dyved," said Manawyddan. "Caswallon knows that, or he would have sent men here before now. But I have no doubt that Math would hold out the hand of friendship to us if we went to Gwynedd. A true friend's hand, not that of one who sought to glorify himself by parading our need."

Pryderi said harshly, "I never will go as a beggar to him whose fellow king I once was," and turned his back upon them all. Later he grew friendly again and merry, indeed so very merry

that that night everybody was glad to get to bed
and so end the strain.

Later, where they lay side by side in the dark,
Rhiannon spoke to her husband. "The boy grows
weary of this life here."

For a little Manawyddan was silent. To hear
what one already knows can be hard. Then he
said, "I have wondered that trouble did not come
upon him before. They are his people who are
gone, the sheep to whom he was shepherd."

"And he loved them. He was so proud, too, of
having made Dyved a kingdom again—it that the
New Tribes had split into petty princedoms. You
did not see him when he came home with his head
high, after taking the Seven Cantrevs of Seissyllwch."

"And now all that is undone."

"Yes, but for awhile he did not realize that. He
is so young; all this new life was like a game to
him, a boy's lark."

"But now his mind, that for awhile was
stunned, is rested. This has been like that other
time, that rest beyond time when the Head of
Bran my brother talked with us and healed us of
our hurts. Your Birds sang to us then. Your Birds,
Rhiannon. Could you not have them sing to Pryderi again and bring him peace?"

She said sadly, "My Birds sing no more. Sometimes I go to meet them in the wood, and they
perch on my hands or rub their beaks against my
face in love. But they make no sound; that dread
night took their voices."

He sighed. "Then there is no help for it. We
must go forth into the world of men again. And

we have been happy here. I would not want to go, even if I trusted Caswallon as far as I tried to make Pryderi think I do."

"I did not think you trusted him. For himself Caswallon would still fear your powers, even though he knows that you could not save Dyved. No man could have."

Manawyddan laughed shortly. "He might not fear me—seeing me so utterly overthrown. But I cannot be sure of that. And whatever happens the boy must not get any ideas into his head about fighting Caswallon. Once many men might have risen to follow us, but not now. For when ill luck has come on a man, who can tell when or if it will leave him? And surely Pryderi and I have shown that the ill luck that was on us in Ireland still clings to us."

"That is not so. You came back to a curse that had waited for me and mine since the night I first slept with Pwyll. The night that he and his men beat Gwawl who had tried to take me from him. I should have known that that doom would fall at last."

"When the sun shines, Lady, it is hard to believe that misfortune will come. But what is done is done; what matters now is what is to come. Since Pryderi will not be content to stay here much longer, and since he and I cannot make any fight for place and power, we would do well to take new names and live quietly among humble men."

"Lord, that will not please Pryderi."

"Yet it must be tried. Let us talk of ways and means."

So, once again, the son of Llyr braced himself for change.

Spring drew near. Every day Pryderi grew more restless. He prowled up and down the lonely hall of Arberth, and looked at the benches where once had sat a host of men. And he seemed to look at their silence and to listen to their emptiness, as if both had been a cry.

The day came at last when he said, with energy, "I cannot stand this. It is like being buried alive. Let us go some place where there are people—people who stay where they belong, and do not get blown away."

Rhiannon, who had been sewing, laid down her work, and Manawyddan, who had been polishing a spear, set it down. Both thought how glad the people of Dyved would have been to stay where they belonged, but neither of them said anything. They knew the soreness that must be in Pryderi's heart; the sick cry that must rise there: *If only I had never mounted the Mound of Arberth . . .*

He spoke again. He said, "Let us go where we can hear a child squalling, or an old woman talking about how to cook beans, or a man boasting about all the other men he has killed in battles he never fought in. Once I thought those three sounds the dullest that ever mauled a man's ears, but now I could love anything that made a noise!"

"It is true that it is very still here," said Kigva. Her bright eyes looked wistful, as if recalling all the live, delightful noisiness that that hall had once held.

She touched her ears, that perched delicately as butterflies under her shining hair. "Indeed, ears, you used to love singing and harping and tale-telling, and the sound of women telling what other women were doing or wearing, but it is little of that you get now."

"If mine do not get something to do soon they will dry up and fall off," grumbled Pryderi.

He walked down the hall again, very fast, and then back up it. Rhiannon looked at Manawyddan, and Manawyddan looked at Rhiannon.

"Indeed," the son of Llyr sighed, "we must not go on like this. The life here is pleasant—or it was—but it is no real trouble, and I am afraid," and he sighed again, "that it is the business of men to have trouble."

"Let us go out and have some," said Pryderi. He threw back his yellow head and hearkened, like a young hound sniffing at the breezes. Longing to hear the fleet hooves of the quarry ahead of him, and the belling of the other hounds beside him.

"We will have it," said Manawyddan. "Men always must." A third time he sighed.

So they left Dyved and went into Logres, that green pleasant land that later was to be taken by the Angles and called England. They came to the town later called Hereford, and there they had a strange mishap. For when they opened the bag of gold that they had brought with them there was nothing in it but dry leaves. Pryderi would have thrown these out in wrath, but his mother stopped him.

"It is still really gold, Son, only the appearance of leaves has been put upon it. This is more of the work of my people."

"Indeed, Mother," said Pryderi disgustedly, "I

am very fond of you, but it is not fond at all I am of any of my other relatives on your side of the house."

Rhiannon gave Manawyddan a wry smile. It said, *How little he dreams that I am the only one of my House who has had anything to do with this.* Husband and wife had planned this small magical trick between them; Caswallon was more likely to hear of rich people than of poor ones.

Aloud she said, "The innkeeper may trust us for a little while, but not long enough for us to go back to Dyved and get more gold."

"And what good would that do? It would turn into more leaves on the way!" Pryderi laughed angrily, but looked a little troubled. Never before had the Lord of Dyved had any reason to worry about debt.

"We could go to Caer Loyu," said Kigva. "Nobody would dare to stop us if we said we were going there."

Pryderi turned upon her sternly. "You are forgetting that your father Gwynn Gloyu is dead, and that your aunts the Nine Witches now rule in Caer Loyu."

"That makes no difference," said Kigva. "When he was alive they ruled there all the same. I know that you do not like my aunts and that they do not like you, but indeed," she added reflectively, "they never like anybody. Even me, of whom they are very fond."

"I will go anywhere and do anything except live with your aunts!" said Pryderi violently.

"There are worse people than my aunts," said Kigva. "They will be glad to see us. They are always glad to have company because it annoys them, and it is so much fun to think of ways to annoy people who annoy them. They are very good hostesses, once you get used to them."

"I will not get used to them!" said Pryderi. "I will not try to!"

"We shall have to learn a trade then," said Manawyddan, "and learn it quickly."

Pryderi stared. "Work?" he said. "For our livings? As if we were not gentlemen born?" Already the New Tribes were learning that kind of pride.

"You wanted trouble," said Manawyddan.

Pryderi digested that, then laughed, "Well," he said, "I have cast the dice and I will play the game out."

They became saddlemakers; it seems unlikely that they knew how to make saddles, but equally unlikely that they knew how to do anything else that ordinary breadwinning men must do.

They only knew how to eat, and they had to find a way to keep on doing that.

At first it did not occur to Pryderi that they could not do anything they had a mind to do. He had seen saddles, so it seemed to him that he ought to be able to make saddles, though naturally his first few attempts might be clumsy. But soon the image of a fine saddle made by himself, that image which had seemed as comfortably near as the house across the lane, flew away like a bird and lit upon a treetop where it sat and cawed at him.

"Indeed," he said, scratching his handsome head, "there seems to be a trick in this. I never thought that there was such power in saddlemakers; it seems strange that they should be able to do anything that I cannot. Perhaps," he added hopefully, "it is like fish swimming or birds flying. There is a knack to it, and if you were born of saddlemakers you have it, but if you were born of queens, like us, you have not got it.

"We were not meant to have it," he ended with conviction.

"We have stomachs," said Manawyddan.

"That is true," sighed Pryderi. And went back to work.

But soon Manawyddan said, "It will be long before our skill equals that of men who have worked at this all their lives. We need some new thing; something to draw folks' eyes to our saddles."

"We can gild them," said Pryderi.

"We can do more than that. There is a stuff called Calch Llassar. I learned the art of its making from Llassar himself, the fiery Giant from the Lake."

All one night Manawyddan stayed up brewing the Calch Llassar. Kigva said, "I have not seen such cauldron-work since I left my aunts the Nine Witches." But neither she nor Pryderi liked the smell, and they soon went to bed.

Rhiannon stayed by the fire, sewing, and Manawyddan said to her, "He was a great craftsman, Llassar. I have seen him make this stuff, and marveled at how he could catch the very blue of the sky in it. I asked him to show me how it was done, and he said, 'Send me a man you trust, and I will teach him. It does not become yourself to get your hands dirtied and your fine clothes spoiled, king's brother.' But I have always found it best to keep knowledge in my own head, so I did my own learning. Though until now the only use I ever made of it was to paint a wooden doll's robe blue for Branwen; she was little then. I can still see her eyes when she first saw that doll."

He paused, and said in wonder, "Yes, I see it. I, who thought I never should be able to see Branwen's face again, save as it looked when Bran dragged her back from that fireplace in Ireland, where her boy died. As it looked at Aber Alaw, where she died. Two sights that burned my heart like fire."

"But now those are only two faces out of all her faces," said Rhiannon. "Out of all the many you remember."

"It is so. I have lived on and been busy with other things; I have not known that I was forgetting her. Yet by that forgetting I have regained her. It is a Mystery."

"Her sorrow was on her, it was not herself. You had to forget it to remember her. She was dearest to you of all, I think; your young sister."

Manawyddan hesitated. "Bran and I were always together; each of us would have felt one-armed without the other. But I never felt such tenderness for Bran as for her. She was loveliness. She was our mother, for there is a mother in all women from the time the girl-baby reaches out her arms for her first doll. And she was our child; we had taught her to walk." And too much came back all at once, and he groaned, "O Bran, brother, why did you have to destroy even her for Caradoc?"

"Because Caradoc was part of him," said Rhiannon. "I know. I never yet have felt as if Pryderi were quite all out of me, though only for nine moons did I carry him safe in my body, and for many years now he has been running about, getting himself into all the kinds of unsafety that he can find. Yet whatever touches him still touches me." And she laid her hand on her breast.

"That is the way of women," said Manawyddan.

The day came when the saddles were ready. Manawyddan and Pryderi showed them in the marketplace. Many came to look, and all who could buy bought, whether they needed saddles or not. For never had there been any saddles like those saddles; the gilt upon them shone golden in the sun, and the blue enamel called Calch Llassar glowed as blue as the sky above it.

By evening there were no golden saddles left.

Manawyddan and Pryderi paid their bills, which must have been many unless, as seems likely, Rhiannon had quietly turned a few dead leaves back into gold pieces. Then they set about making more saddles.

These too were sold as soon as they were made. And so it went with the next batch, and the next and the next. People came from far away to buy those saddles. Everybody was in love with them, and anybody who was not would have been thought blind in at least one eye.

But the other saddlemakers in Hereford did not

sell anything at all. They did not like that, and they held a meeting about it.

"We might ask the older man to tell us how to make the Calch Llassar," said one, but not very hopefully.

"He would not tell us," said another flatly.

"We could try to make him tell," suggested a third. "We could do things to him until he did," he added.

"That would hurt him, and be unlawful," said yet another. "It would likewise be wrong. We are honest men, and honest tradesmen. We cannot do anything that is not law-abiding, and proper."

"No," they all said sadly; and though they had been gloomy before, deeper gloom came and wrapped itself about them like a cloak.

"A man's knowledge is his own," the thoughtful one continued, "and nobody has a right to deprive him of it. But our trade was ours, and he has deprived us of that. It always has been lawful for decent men to poke a spear into a wolf, and this man who makes the Calch Llassar is more dangerous to us than any wolf. It would be decent and law-abiding of us to kill him."

These words seemed to light a torch in each man. Their slumped bodies straightened, their eyes gleamed, and their ears listened.

"Would it?" they said happily.

Only one man objected. "We will have to kill the young man too. And what about the women? It seems a pity to kill them, for they are good-looking."

"It would not be sensible to do anything else," said the plan-maker, "for they may know something about the Calch Llassar. Besides, they probably would bear us ill will for killing their men, and a woman's ill will is unlucky."

"Then we will kill them all," said the others. "Though indeed we would not do it if it were not right, for we are decent, law-abiding men."

By then it was nearly dawn, so they decided that it would be better to wait until the next night to do anything. They all went home to bed, and their thoughts that had been heavy as stones were light as feathers, and their sleep that had been uneasy and haunted was sound and sweet.

Only one man could not go to sleep, the man who had objected.

He thought, *When we go to kill them, we must all go, so I must go too. We will certainly kill them, but since they are all four healthy, able-bodied people they may kill some of us first.*

They might even kill me.

We are many; there are many others they could kill besides me. I have no way of knowing that it would be me.

I have no way of knowing that it would not.

I may get hurt, even if I do not get killed.

Indeed, he groaned, *why could not all this have been settled peaceably, without such a fuss. If they only knew that we were going to kill them they would run away. Anybody would run away . . .*

Like lightning blazing across a dark sky, the thought smote him: they could know, for he could tell them.

The thought burned him like fever, it froze him like ice, but he could not get away from it. In the end he rose and went out into the morning twilight. He went stealthily, by back ways and strange ways. He had borrowed his woman's hooded cloak, so that nobody would know him if he were seen: and indeed he devoutly hoped that nobody was the only person who would see him.

He came to the door of Manawyddan's house and knocked.

Kigva and Rhiannon were already getting breakfast, and it was Kigva who answered that knock. When she saw him her mouth and eyes became three round moons, and while she stood and stared he tried to back away, but Rhiannon called from within, "What is it, girl?"

"It is a woman with whiskers!" said Kigva. And she became a leap and a pounce and a spring, and what she pounced on was those whiskers. The man yelped.

Rhiannon came to them, and her eyes were hard.

"Explain yourself," she said. "You who would sneak into decent women's kitchens pretending to be another woman."

He explained.

Rhiannon called Manawyddan, and he came and listened, and asked a few questions, which the man answered.

"You will run away?" the man asked eagerly. "You will run away?"

"I do not know yet," said Manawyddan. "I must take counsel with my son. But if we stay, and if we kill anybody, it will not be you."

"It will be anybody Pryderi can lay hands on,"

Kigva said, her eyes flashing, "once he has heard this."

The man fled.

But when Pryderi heard, he did not seem angry. He merely cocked his head on one side and smiled. His eyes shone and his teeth shone.

"Let us kill these people," he said joyously, "instead of letting them kill us."

"It would not be wise," said Manawyddan.

"It would be great fun," said Pryderi. "I have been getting very bored with all this work. Let us do it," he urged.

"We will not," said Manawyddan. "We will take what baggage we can carry, and leave this town today."

Pryderi's mouth fell open. "You mean that we will let them make *us* run away?"

"We will make ourselves run away," said Manawyddan. "It is only just. We have hurt their trade, and they must live."

"We must live too," said Pryderi. "You have said so often enough."

"We can live somewhere else," said Manawyddan. "In some place where we have not made enemies."

10

The Gold Shoemakers

They came to another town, a town that the *Mabinogi* leaves unnamed. It says only that they came there.

"What craft shall we take here?" asked Pryderi. "Let it not be saddlemaking," he begged. "I am sick of saddles. Who needs saddles? A man should sit on what the Gods gave him to sit on. That is well padded enough."

"Let us make shields," said Manawyddan.

"Can we?" Pryderi stroked his chin, for he suddenly remembered that it took time to learn how to do things. "Do we know anything about how to make shields?"

"We will try," said Manawyddan.

They tried, and presently they succeeded. Pryderi never found it very interesting work, but he said that at least it was better than making saddles.

"Though it is a man's work to carry a shield, not to make one," he grumbled.

But it is true that to learn to do a thing well takes time, and the townspeople kept on buying from the local shieldmakers. From the men who knew their trade, the men they were used to. The newcomers could not make a living; they tried to undersell their competitors, but found that if they did so they would not have enough profit left to live.

There came a week when they ate lightly, and the next week they ate more lightly still.

"Maybe there is some good in saddles after all," said Pryderi. "Leather is a little like meat." He rubbed his flattened belly and said, "It is hollow I am. Hollow as the big tree that the birds used to nest in at home."

Manawyddan said, "We need some new thing. Something to draw the customers' eyes."

That night he stayed up to make some more of the Calch Llassar. He painted all his shields blue, and then showed them, glowing like great jewels, in the marketplace.

After that it seemed to rain blue shields and to hail them and snow them. If a man did not have a blue shield, he himself was blue, and he made haste to get one, and so get back his own right color. And if by any chance he did still like his old shield and did not want to part with it, his woman was blue, and could not be comforted until he got himself a fine new blue shield, and looked as smart as the men of other women.

But the local shieldmakers were bluer than anybody else, for nobody bought anything of them any more.

Rhiannon said to Manawyddan, "Lord, what if that happens which happened before?"

"Let it," said Pryderi comfortably. There was a large haunch of beef before him, and as he spoke he cut a large slice off it. "If the other shieldmakers want to kill us we can always kill them."

"If we do, Caswallon and his men will hear of it," Manawyddan looked troubled. "You are right to have fears, Lady; but it seemed that I had no choice."

"Well, perhaps nothing will happen for awhile," said Kigva. And she looked around the house at the new pots and cups that she and Rhiannon had just bought, and at everything else that they had bought and done to make the place comfortable and handsome.

"It is pleasant here," she said. "I should like to stay."

"You shall," said Pryderi. "Who would dare to drive us out?"

"They did at the last place . . ."

But Pryderi stuffed a big juicy bite of the beef into her mouth and silenced her.

Time passed. Manawyddan and Pryderi made shields as fast as they could, and sold them even faster. They had far more orders than they could meet.

One day a young servingman came to the house. It chanced that he found Rhiannon alone, for Kigva was helping the men to paint the shields.

"Woman of the house," he said, "let you tell your man to make haste with my master's shield. He wants it by tomorrow noon."

"Who is your master?" said Rhiannon.

"Huw the son of Cradoc."

Rhiannon thought a moment. "There are several ahead of him. We cannot have his shield ready before the third noon from now. But I will speak to my man. We will do what we can."

The young man looked offended. Huw the son of Cradoc was a chieftain, and one of the richest men in the cantrev; few said no to him.

"You must do better than that, woman. My master must have his shield by tomorrow noon."

"Even if men who ordered their shields before him wait for theirs? That is not the way we treat our customers, young man." But then suddenly Rhiannon checked herself; her eyes narrowed. "Why does your master want the shield so soon, boy. What has put such haste on him?"

Her eyes were eyes no longer. They were spears, they were arrows, plunging into his. They were inside him, in the depths of him, and against his will his mouth opened. His tongue did her bidding, not his own.

"Because after that he cannot get it, Lady. Because tomorrow night the other shieldmakers and all their kin and friends will come here. They will burn this house over your heads, and if any of you stick those heads out they will cut them off."

"Well," said Rhiannon, "I cannot altogether blame them. Go now and give your master the message I gave you. You will tell him nothing else."

And indeed, the moment her eyes left his, that young man clean forgot that he had told her anything at all except what his master had bidden him tell her. He felt only annoyance because these unreasonable people were going to get killed before they had done what Huw the son of Cradoc wanted. And a little uneasiness for fear Huw might blame him.

But whatever the son of Cradoc may have done, Pryderi the son of Pwyll was soon raging.

"This is not to be endured from these boors! Let us go out now—tonight—and hunt them out like the treacherous rats they are! Let us butcher them!"

"Then we will be the lawbreakers," said Manawyddan. "It will be Caswallon's chance to put us out of the way quickly and quietly, pretending that he does not recognize us."

For a little Pryderi was silent, breathing hard. "What shall we do then? Run away again? *Again?*"

"We will go to another town," said Manawyddan. And so they did.

Again we are not told where that town was. Likely it was farther from the heartland of the Island of the Mighty than the one they had just left, for there Manawyddan seems to have feared the nearness of Caswallon. Perhaps it lay somewhat nearer the blue hills of Wales and the wilderness that once had been Dyved.

Wherever it was, they came there; and Manawyddan said to Pryderi, "What craft shall we take? It is your turn to choose."

"Anything you like so long as we know it," said Pryderi. "I am not in favor of learning how to do anything new; we have to learn too often."

"Not so," said Manawyddan. "Let us make shoes. For I notice that the shoemakers here are peaceable-looking folk, and that there are not many of them. I do not believe that they will have any stomach for killing. I am a little tired," he said, "of people that are trying to kill me."

"I am not," said Pryderi. "What I am tired of—very tired of—is not trying to kill them."

"Son," said Rhiannon, "your father is right. Here we must try to keep out of trouble."

"I need exercise," said Pryderi. "I cannot get it sitting in a shop. I need a fight. And I do not know the singlest, smallest thing about shoemaking."

"I do," said Manawyddan, "and I will teach you to stitch. We will not try to dress the leather, we will buy it already dressed, and then cut the shoes out of it."

"Indeed," said Pryderi, "I would rather be cutting the heads off those people that keep running us out of town." But he subsided then; that was his last protest.

The *Mabinogi* says that Manawyddan bought the best leather that was to be had in town, and that he found the best goldsmith in town, and had him make gilded clasps for the shoes. He watched that making until he knew the method of it. Then he gilded, not only the clasps, but the shoes themselves. They shone like gold; no shoes so beautiful were ever seen in the Island of the Mighty save those that Gwydion made, the golden-tongued son of Don, when he too played shoemaker in order to trick sun-bright Arianrhod and so get a name for that little son of theirs whom she hated and he loved. But all that befell in later times.

Kigva and Rhiannon marveled at that first pair of golden shoes. They held them up this way and that way and several other ways, and were delighted and dazzled by them.

Pryderi whistled. "I would hate to be in the

shoes of the other shoemakers once we have a good stock of these. They are a better reason for killing us than anybody has had yet."

"They are beautiful," said Kigva. Her eyes could not leave them. "Too beautiful to make anybody angry," She tried them on.

"I hope so," said Rhiannon. But though her voice was doubtful, her eyes could not leave the shoes either.

If that town stayed the same at the top, it became brilliant at the bottom. It flashed as though all the stars in heaven had fallen and were going about its streets in pairs, with a person sprouting from each pair.

Feet glowed and gleamed, they flashed and sparkled. They twinkled like fireflies, they moved sedately like the moon, they strode ponderously and stately like the sun marching triumphantly toward noon.

They were golden, and so was the waterfall that poured into the purses of Manawyddan and Pryderi.

None of the other shoemakers sold anything, and none of them liked that.

But for four moons the Gold Shoemakers made their golden shoes in peace. Then a woman came to the shop after nightfall, and found Manawyddan alone. She said to him, "If you will make me a pair of golden shoes for nothing, I will tell you something."

Manawyddan stroked his chin.

"Something more precious than gold? That would be something indeed," said he. "What is it?"

"When I have the shoes I will tell you."

Manawyddan stroked his chin some more.

"You will get the shoes when I get the knowledge," he said. "But I will measure your feet now. Once the shoes are made we will both lose if you do not get them, for it is unlikely that they will fit anybody else."

"Well, do not be too long about it," said she, and he did not like the look in her eye when she said that.

He told the others of the bargain he had made, and Rhiannon rose at once.

"I will begin packing," she said with resignation. "Kigva, do you see to our clothes and the linens. I will take the kitchen shelves."

"Indeed and indeed," lamented Kigva, "I am tired of getting used to new houses. We have no sooner thought out the best way to place the pots and pans, and I have no sooner learned to remember where they all are, than we are running away again."

"I am tired of traveling! I am tired of being run out of town! I am tired of towns!" And she sat down and wept.

"That looks pleasant," said Rhiannon, "and I would like to do it too. But this is not the time for it; we must pack."

But Pryderi put his arms around Kigva and comforted her.

"You shall have a head off one of these boors to put in every pot," he said tenderly. "And another to put in every pan. You shall not have to run away anymore."

"Only once more," said Manawyddan. "Towns are no place for us; that is clear. We could buy a farm, but we would be almost as lonely there as we were in Dyved, and the land never would be really our land. Let us go back to Dyved and farm there," said he.

For a breath's space Pryderi and Kigva looked at him blankly; then a light dawned in their faces, like dawn coming up over the midsummer marshes, faint and cool and sweet, the promise of a fresher, clearer day.

"Dyved—!" said Pryderi. And a hundred memories rang in his voice, of big things and little things, of trees climbed and fish caught, of glad homecomings and eager goings forth. All the memories of a lifetime, of a life that had been good.

"Indeed," he breathed softly, "there is not a better place in all the world to go back to. Dyved . . ."

"Indeed," said Kigva, smiling through her tears, "it is a nice place, Dyved. Nobody ever ran us out of it, and nobody ever will, for there is nobody left there to do it."

But Rhiannon was not smiling, and her face looked white and still as some beautiful, snow-covered country caught fast in the chill grip of winter. Her eyes seemed to see far spaces, and her voice had the sound of wind; of a cold and far-off wind.

"You have got what you have played for, Husband," she said, "and what I have wanted too, but it may be that it is not wise. We will go back to Dyved, for that is the fate that is on us, but Something may be waiting for us there."

11

The Trap

In the springtime they came back to Dyved, and
the land lay fair and still before them, and the
Three Birds of Rhiannon flew before them, their
wings shining in the sun.

Once Rhiannon went apart and held up her
hands and called them. They came and lit upon
her fingers, and she spoke to them, in some
strange sweet chirping tongue. And with chirps as
sweet they answered; for the first time since that
dreadful night they made sounds, although they
did not sing.

But when Rhiannon came back to the others,
her face was white and grave, and when they
asked her if she had learned anything, she shook
her head.

"Nothing that I can tell in the tongue of men.
They do not know all, and I cannot recognize, in
their tongue, the name they speak. It is a great
name, it casts a great shadow—a twilight in the
heart, and a stillness all around, as though Earth
Herself, our Mother, hearing it, held Her breath
and was afraid."

"But this I know: The Birds said clearly, *'Be
watchful. Be watchful. Watchful . . .'"*

The Birds left them when they came to Arberth,

to that quiet palace waiting with the golden sun upon it, and its lonely chambers all dark and still within.

They built a cooking fire, and pastured the cow that they had brought with them. They tried to talk, but the silence seemed to drown their voices. Those desolate chambers seemed to have a dead feeling that they had never had before, as if the voices of all those people who had been violently swept away from their life here cried mutely from the walls. Cried for warmth and breath, and all that they had been deprived of.

Toward evening that silence was broken, shattered by a great belling of hounds.

Pryderi ran out through the palace doors and was all but knocked down by a rush of upward-leaping paws, and upward-leaping bodies, and frantically licking tongues.

"It is my dogs!" he cried. "My dogs!"

He patted this one's head, and scratched that one under the chin, and another behind the left ear, and yet another behind the right ear. He patted and scratched and tickled, and they leapt and licked and wagged their tails as if they would wag them off.

"I have come back to you, my darlings!" he exulted. "I have come back." And his eye beamed with tenderness and pity for them, who had thought that they had lost him.

Then suddenly he sobered; looked down upon them with an eye grown stern. "Indeed, it was not I that ran off and left you. I had not seen you for years before I went. You must have run away."

The dogs whined. They looked back uneasily

toward the dark forest from which they had come. Their hackles rose and they whined again and shivered, and crouched down as close to Pryderi as they could get, looking up at him with great troubled eyes, as if trying to tell him something.

Rhiannon said quietly, "The dogs did not run away, Son. They were taken . . ."

She and the others had followed him out, and Pryderi swung round to her, silent for a breath's space. Then he said, quickly and sharply, "But they have come back!"

His words were a statement, but his eyes were questions, bright and eager, and Kigva slipped her hand into his. She breathed softly, round-eyed, "Do you suppose that some day the people could come back too?"

Rhiannon shook her head. "Anything could happen. But I do not think that that will. Build no hopes upon it, children."

"But the dogs were not killed! They have come back. They are here!"

Both young people had spoken together, and Pryderi added, looking down at the dogs and scratching his head, "But where have they been all this time? And how did they get back from there?"

"Ask those questions of Whatever took them, Son. But no—I pray to the Mothers that you may never get the chance."

Something in Rhiannon's voice brought back the silence. As if a great cold finger had been laid suddenly upon each of their hearts . . .

Then one of the dogs whined again, and Pryderi stooped to pat him and said magnificently, "Be still. I will not let anything get you again."

All the dogs believed him; he even believed himself. They looked up at him thankfully, and their tails wagged again, and their panting tongues lolled so red and happily and gratefully that they too seemed to be wagging.

In their bed that night Manawyddan said to his lady, "I hope that the dogs will stay. Or be allowed to stay. That will mean much to the boy."

She said, "I do not know what I hope. They may have been sent back for a purpose."

"Well, we must be careful," said Manawyddan.

The dogs stayed, and Pryderi went hunting with them, and brought home many a dinner. They were the same as always; wherever they had been, that place of Mystery had not changed them. It takes a great deal to change the loving simplicity of dogs.

The leaves reddened and fell. Winter came howling down from the blue mountains; whitened all the land. Spring came, and the woods foamed white again, this time with hawthorne bloom; and still nothing happened. By then everybody was less careful. People who walk warily at first, half-expecting a monster to pop out from behind every bush, and a happening to be hiding grimly in every corner, could not help but be very surprised if, a year later, there should be anything but emptiness or another bush behind a bush. Or anything but shadows, and maybe a cobweb or two, in a corner.

So summer found them: happy and unsuspicious.

Then the rains began. They lashed those windswept heights where once the Holy Stones had stood; they drenched the deep green woods and made mud of the brown breast of Earth the Mother. Pryderi let the dogs into the great hall, and there he and they padded restlessly, tired of having nothing to do. He and Kigva quarreled, though they soon made it up again.

"But it will not stay made up long," said Kigva to Rhiannon, "unless this rain stops and he can get out of the house."

"Maybe this is my business," said Rhiannon. "He is acting like a little boy again. Shall I tell him so?"

Kigva considered. "No. It is our quarrel. Do you and Father look the other way, and let us fight it out in peace."

But in the morning the rain had stopped. Pryderi and Manawyddan rose early and went out to hunt, the dogs leaping happily around them.

For awhile they got nothing but muddy feet. Mist steamed around them, they could seldom see their way, but they were free of the house, and that freedom seemed good.

The morning wore; the mists vanished, but the sun did not come out. The sky was gray and shining. Not a breath of wind stirred, not a leaf moved.

"It is very still," said Pryderi. "I wish the dogs would find something."

Manawyddan too had been thinking that it was very still. He said, "Give the dogs time."

But they tramped on and on and nothing happened.

The sun, the golden lady of day, fought to pierce that silver veil. As a man may see his own face dimly mirrored in deep water, so moon-pale images of her glimmered here and there among the trees. One seemed to be sinking straight ahead of them, shining in the green dusk.

Manawyddan said in wonder, "I have seen such sights beside the Usk, but never this far west."

But at that very moment the dogs set up a great barking. Like a flight of thrown spears they shot forward, and with a gleeful shout Pryderi plunged after them. Manawyddan followed, running as fast as he could.

The race ended as suddenly as it had begun. The dogs stopped, growling, before a thick green bush. For a last dizzy moment, as he ran, Manawyddan thought he saw that mock moon sinking, in a flash of white light, behind that same bush. Then he stood beside Pryderi, panting and rubbing his eyes.

The dogs turned and ran back to the men. Their hair bristled; it stood straight up on their backs. They were afraid, desperately afraid; they who never before had shown fear of any quarry.

Pryderi laughed. "Let us go up to that bush, and see what is hiding in it." His eyes shone. Excitement was on him, like a kind of drunkenness.

He sprang toward the bush.

Like lightning a huge gleaming body leapt from its green shelter; leapt and was gone.

But not far. It turned and stood, its small evil eyes flaming, its terrible curved tusks ready. It was a wild boar, a pure white boar, and there was something awful in that whiteness. A chill as of a color (or a colorlessness) too white to have any place in all nature. To the son of Llyr it seemed the chilling, repulsive whiteness of death.

Pryderi did not feel it. His face flamed with delight. "At him, Gwythur! After him, Kaw! Get him, Fflam! Take him, my darlings!"

Always before they had leapt at that command, joyous and arrow-swift. But now they shrank and cowered; they looked up at him piteously, as if to say, "We would love to kill him. We would love to please you. But we dare not—we dare not . . ."

He was inexorable. "At him! Are you dogs, or are you mice?"

They could not bear that; they charged.

The boar stood and fought them, savagely. He ripped up one on his tusks, and the others wavered, then charged him again.

Pryderi, seeing his dog killed, charged too, yelling with fury. Again Manawyddan ran as fast as he could, fear tearing his heart, striving to reach his son before Pryderi and the boar met.

The dogs were still snarling and leaping, but the white boar seemed to be playing with them. To be waiting for their master.

Not ten feet from him, Manawyddan caught up with Pryderi. Side by side, they rushed on. Then and not until then, the boar turned and fled. Was off, incredibly swift, incredibly, deathly white, into the forest.

Pryderi sped after him, shouting to the dogs. Manawyddan was left behind again. He could not keep up with them; his legs had not the springy swiftness of youth. But he was tough; they could not shake him off.

The hounds ran, the men ran, and always before them, like a flash of pale, cold light, was the white boar.

Often, even in the heat of the chase, something like a door had flashed open inside the son of Llyr, and he had felt a queer kind of oneness with the quarry. A pity for the thing that must die to feed him. But now he felt only loathing. That white beast was hideous to him, he would have gagged over its flesh, yet he would have rejoiced to see it die. It was a thing that should not be.

He was running too fast to think. His body ached, his ears were filled with the singing of the blood in his bursting head. From very far away, almost as if from another world, he heard the quavering, frightened, yet still fierce baying of the hounds: heard Pryderi urging them on. His swimming eyes saw the coldly gleaming boar flashing in and out of a green mist. Trees . . .

The trees must be running too, their very roots sliding frantically beneath the earth, striving to get away from the chill of that beast that was too white to be a natural thing . . .

He could not see where he was going; he could not see anything clearly. Every breath tore his chest. But he must keep on; he must not lose Pryderi.

The boar had stopped. He was getting bigger. His whiteness was glistening, shimmering, expanding into a sparkling ball . . . It was not the boar. It was that fallen moon, and it had grown as big as a hill.

He was climbing it. He could still hear Pryderi and the dogs ahead of him, and he called out to stop them.

"Pyrderi! Pryderi!"

Then he saw it. The opening in that white, shining hill. Like a black mouth it yawned beneath the massive, intricately carved stone lintel.

Snow-white the boar flashed across that black mouth and dived into it; dwindled and grew small in its darkness, a racing point of white light.

Baying loudly, the hounds plunged in after it. Like a mouth indeed, the darkness seemed to swallow them up. Pryderi would have leapt in after them, but Manawyddan caught his arm.

They stood there, like men waking from a dream; realizing suddenly that they never had seen this place before.

Pryderi whispered shakily, "It was never here before."

They looked up at the gray shining sky; it was the same. They looked down, and saw that beneath their feet was neither grass nor earth, but pebbles of white quartz. A solid mass of them, that covered the whole hillside.

What hillside? And whence had these white stones come?

They looked back toward the dark mouth of the passage.

No bark came from it, no sound at all. The dogs must be lost in those depths, beyond light, beyond sight, beyond sound.

Silence seemed to creep out of that black mouth, like exhaled breath. To creep up around them and cover them, like a rising mist.

They turned and ran uphill.

At the top they stopped, panting, and gasped, but not for lack of breath.

They stood upon the top of the Gorsedd Arberth, of that gateway between the worlds.

"We have been led here," Manawyddan said slowly. "Blinded and led."

Pryderi did not seem to hear. He looked back the way they had come, and his eyes were both fierce and troubled.

"The dogs," he muttered. "The dogs."

"Let us wait here a little," said Manawyddan. "This is a high place. There could be no better spot for spying them if they come out again."

So they looked and listened, with the green waste that had been Dyved outspread below them, but they saw nothing and heard nothing. No bird flew across the sky; no wind stirred a leaf.

Restlessness came on Pryderi; settled on him and grew.

"Lord," he said at last. "I am going to go into the hill and find the dogs. Or at least find out what has happened to them."

"Are you mad?" said Manawyddan. "Whoever it is that cast a spell over this land has opened up the hillside and entrapped the dogs."

"I know that, but this is the Mound of the Testing. This may be my test."

"It is a trap. You said that this passage was never here before, but it has been. Through it the first King of Dyved was taken to his burial chamber, and then his Mound was built over him and covered with white quartz to make it shine like the moon, like the tombs of Irish Kings. Then for ages it was sealed, and strangers drove out his people, and the white stones were carried off or covered with grass. That lost entrance may well be what common men mean when they speak of this place as a gateway between the worlds."

"It is not lost now, but found." Pryderi pulled impatiently at the hand that again had grasped his arm.

"It is found. Death has opened his jaws. Would you walk into them?"

Pryderi tried to speak patiently. "You do not understand, second-father. You were not born here, you do not come of the blood of the Lords of Dyved. I do, and I accept the destiny that is laid on me."

"I understand that you would throw your life away. Think of Kigva and your mother."

"I do. These last years have not been easy for them. Maybe if I go into the hill the spell will be broken—everything put back as it was before. Our people freed."

"If they live. Boy, that is a fair dream, but it is a dream."

Pryderi pulled his arm free. "In any case I cannot give up my dogs like this."

Manawyddan's hand dropped; he understood. This boy who had brought disaster upon a whole people could never knowingly forsake even a dog. The guilt that for years had crouched deep down under all his gaiety had not kept him from driving these poor beasts, too, to their doom. But that driving had added the last straw to the old load. Not again could Pryderi bear to walk unscathed while those who had trusted him perished.

Sadly the son of Llyr watched that straight young figure stride down the hill. "Loyalty is strong in you," he said softly. "You are a true son of kings, even if not of those you think sired you."

He thought of Bran, and of Beli their mother's brother, Beli who had been called the Mighty. *They would have been proud of you, boy, though they would have thought you a fool.* But then black realization smote him, burning through the last threads of that web of glamour that had numbed him too. Loss drowned pride. He writhed in such agony of soul as he had not known since Bran fell. But his training held; his mind was still his master. No use to try to follow the boy now; no earthly power could save Pryderi. If help ever were to reach him, it must come from the free. Not from one who shared his doom.

He knew that waiting was useless, but he waited. The day wore. The sun set, in a sky that seemed to hurt the watching man's eyes; flaming and blood-splashed, as though from a whole world's death.

He sat quietly under its rage, still as the stones around him.

Night came; the moon rose. And still Manawyddan waited . . .

He said to himself at last, *This is foolishness. You know that there is no more hope.*

Down below, the women must be waiting in fear; knowing that if something had not happened their men would have come home by now. Unkind to keep them waiting; unkind, too, to tell them what he must tell them . . .

He went down from the Gorsedd. He drew his

cloak around him, for a wind had risen. It whined about him as he went; cold, colder than any summer wind he had ever felt. Like an ice-cold breath it smote him as he passed that black mouth that had opened in the hillside; that doorway that loomed dark even through the darkness of night.

Manawyddan glanced once at that opening. He thought dully, *Why has it not closed? Its work is done. Can He that waits inside be fool enough to think that I will still give up the game and come in to Him?*

Then bitter laughter seemed to ring inside his head: his own. *What game have I to give up? What good have I done Dyved, in all the years since He laid it waste? What good can I do my son? My son! My son!*

He went on. That is all a man can do: go on.

He saw the lights of Arberth. They streamed out to meet him, for the great doors stood open.

He went into the hall. Rhiannon sat there, sewing, Kigva sleeping at her knee. He had only a breath's space in which to think that that sleep must have been mercifully induced, either by magic or by herbs, for then Rhiannon saw him. Gladness sprang into her eyes, opened there like a flower. She jumped up, her lips parting to speak his name, her arms going out to him.

And then she saw that he was alone, and all her gladness withered.

Her arms dropped, her face froze. Her eyes became spears piercing him, though her voice was only a whisper. *"Where is he that left here with you?"*

Manawyddan braced himself. He had expected

pain enough from the sight of her pain. He saw now that he was to have an even more bitter cup to drink.

"Lady," he said, "this is what happened."

She listened, her face whitening until it grew as white as death. All the life that drained out of it seemed to burn in her eyes. They flamed; they blazed. They were not Rhiannon's eyes, but only the eyes of Pryderi's mother, and behind her of all that vast long line of mothers, scaly and furred, hairy and hairless, that have been robbed of their young since time began. Manawyddan wished with all his heart that she were still Rhiannon, his Rhiannon, for he had his own grief, and he was very tired. Stupid with fatigue, he groped for words to reach her, to bring her back; at least to comfort her a little.

He ended, "Lady, do not give up hope. For you know, better than we who are earth-born, that it is unlikely that he has died an ordinary death."

Quick as lightning, and as terrible, her wrath lashed at him. "Man without honor, without courage! A bad comrade you have been, and a good comrade you have lost!"

As flame darts over dry leaves she darted past him, and was gone.

He followed her out into the night; he cried her name. "Rhiannon, Rhiannon!" But he caught only a glimpse of her, a tall slender shape vanishing into the rising mists.

He still followed, still calling desperately, "Rhiannon! Rhiannon!" But he was spent and dizzy and his whole body ached; and she was fresh, and of a less weighty make than the women born into our world. He lost her in those ever-thickening mists. Bushes caught at him spitefully, trees thrust themselves in his way. A huge trunk struck him; knocked all the breath out of his body. He fell; rose only to run round and round helplessly, blindly, like a man in a maze. For how long he never knew . . .

With an earsplitting, earthrending crash, thunder blasted the night. The black sky shuddered away from the sizzling, titanic blade of fiery light that seared it.

When Manawyddan's head cleared, the mists had lifted. The moon shone down with a ghostly gentleness. From far to the west came a sad, sweet crying. Three birds were flying seaward, the moon silvering their feathers, the white, the green, and the gold.

The Birds of Rhiannon, singing their farewell to the world of men!

He understood. The Enemy had foreseen that Rhiannon would seek Pryderi. He had sent the mists and the maze-Illusion that Manawyddan might not stop her. The dark opening in the hillside was closed now. That black mouth had swallowed her, the mouthful for which it had waited.

Rhiannon. Rhiannon, my beloved!

With bowed head and stooped shoulders the son of Llyr walked back to Arberth, where this time she would not be waiting. He walked like a very old man, and he felt as if all the weight of all the mountains of the world lay upon his heart.

12

The Son of Llyr Goes On

He came back into the Hall of Arberth, and again he came alone.

The fog had come before him. Only the red embers of the dying fire glowed sickly, faintly, through the mists that stalked the hall like gliding shadow-shapes.

Kigva still slept. Her emptied body, lying there, was no more than another shadow.

He sat down heavily, crouching over those red embers. He felt like a man who sits amid the wastes of winter in the farthest north, in that dread place where sea ends and ice begins. Alone forever in sunless darkness and everlasting cold.

The Mothers alone knew which he grieved for most: for the man whom he had loved as much as Bran had loved Caradoc, or for the woman who had been friend and lover.

Rhiannon and Pryderi. Pryderi and Rhiannon.

O Bran and Branwen! Was it not enough that I had to lose you? I should not have had to lose these two as well. O Mothers, no man should have to bear this twice!

He had known spring and summer, and mighty winds had come and felled the great trees, and lashed all the flowers to death. He had known the chill of loneliness that is greater than the chill of death, since death at least must wipe out loneliness. For the dead are many, and at worst there is no loneliness in sleep.

He had known late summer, with its golden warmth, its tender delight in watching youth when one is no longer torn by the fierce confusing energies of youth. But now once again the trees were stripped and down, and all was over. He was back again in the great cold.

Yet the Enemy who had taken these loved ones, being beyond death, might not deal in the death we know. He had said that to Rhiannon, and it was true.

Yet how can that help you, son of Llyr? How can you, a man, fight with a God? With a God you cannot see?

There was no way; none. Hope was only a mockery.

O Pryderi, should I have gone with you after all? Then at least we would all have been together . . .

But he knew in his heart that that, not this, would have been surrender, flight. He would have given his life to save Pryderi, but he could not throw it away. It was not in the son of Llyr to waste anything.

Pryderi had comforted himself with dreams of a capricious, ruthlessly testing Power that in the end might reward courage. Manawyddan had no such belief. An unearthly Power might be good or evil, but it would be no child-brain, wasting stupendous force in cruel tricks.

Yet in evil there is always weakness. Wisdom is

above malice, above vengeance. Even on earth the
highest druids taught that. Even beyond earth a
Power that cherished such passions could not be
invulnerable, might overreach Itself . . .

But how could such as He overreach Himself so
far as to come within a mortal's reach? A baby
cannot knock down a man.

Well, hope might be a mockery, but a man
cannot live without hope, even if it be only the
paltry hope of getting his dinner in the evening.
And in evil there is weakness.

Kigva stirred and moaned. Her hand groped
beside her, and Manawyddan's eyes closed in sudden sick pain. She thought herself in bed, with
Pryderi beside her.

Her eyes opened, stared blankly around the
great hall, then wildly. She saw him, and her
whole face glowed.

"You have come back, Lord! But Pryderi—where
is Pryderi?" Her voice quivered and broke, like
that of a child staring into a great darkness. She
had seen that he was alone.

Manawyddan braced himself again. She too must
be told . . .

"Where is Pryderi? Where is Rhiannon?"
Kigva's voice rose sharply, as if any sound, even
the sound of her own speech that told her nothing, were better than waiting. This waiting that
strained toward knowledge as toward a monstrous,
unimaginable birth.

"Where is he? Where were you? You did not
come, and you did not come—and the night grew
darker and darker, and I grew more and more
afraid. Until she made me lie down and stroked

my head with her hands. But she has made me
sleep too long . . . where is she? Where is *he?*"

Manawyddan thought of Rhiannon's hands;
those white hands that were full of little magics,
small sweet magics of her womanhood, and of
others, little wonders left over from that Bright
World where she had been born. Was she back in
that world now? Or in some other?

Rhiannon, Rhiannon, where are you?

Kigya said again, "Where are they? Where is
Pryderi?"

"Child, I do not know."

He told her all he did know, and now and then
she broke into his tale with questions, the questions of the suddenly grief-stricken, that try to find
a way for truth not to be true. And then she wept.

She wept, the daughter of Gwynn Gloyu, as if
she could wash away all that had happened, and
float Pryderi back to her on that flood of tears. As
only the young can weep, remembering, if uncon-
sciously, how enough tears once brought gifts or
mercy.

She wept as if she did not care whether she
lived or died.

Manawyddan made breakfast at last, and
brought her some, but though by then she had
wept until she could weep no more, she would not
eat. She only sat silent, staring into nothingness,
and sometimes, as the day wore, she looked at him
when she thought he did not know it, and then
she shuddered.

*I am alone with this man, who has lost his
woman as I have lost my man. We are far away
from any other men or women. Anyone would say*

*that we ought to comfort each other . . . I cannot.
I will not! O Mothers! O Pryderi! Pryderi!*

She saw, not Manawyddan himself, but only a man.

He saw her sight of him. He thought wearily, *This is what comes of the ways of the New Tribes. In the old times, in Harlech, no girl would have thought that a man could enjoy her unless she shared that joy. Had we not grief enough without this?*

It hurt him that this woman who for years had been as his own child could fear him.

He stopped in front of her, too far away to touch her. He looked at her until her eyes rose to meet his. Afraid or not, she had plenty of fighting blood in her.

"Lady," he said, "you do wrong if you fear me. I declare to you that if I were in the dawn of youth I would keep faith with Pryderi, who was as a son to me. You shall have all the friendship that is in my power to give, and nothing else from me, so long as this sorrow is on us."

So quaintly and formally the *Mabinogi* says he spoke to her, and perhaps in no other way could he have reached her. She looked at him, a long, still look. Then she smiled at him, suddenly and brightly and fondly, as a relieved and repentant child might smile at the person who has promised not to hurt it.

"Indeed, Lord, that is what I would have thought you would do, if I had been thinking of you yourself at all. I am sorry!"

"Child, it is forgotten. But we cannot stay here. Alone and without dogs, I am not hunter enough to feed us. Would you like to go to the Witches at Caer Loyu?"

"No," said Kigva, and her lip quivered. "They would tell me that I am well rid of Pryderi, and I could not bear that. Not now! Lord, let me stay with you."

"That is what I hoped you would say," said Manawyddan. And she sprang up and kissed him, and they were as good friends again as ever they had been.

So they left that haunted land where every place spoke of Pryderi and Rhiannon. Where the silence was so loud that it rang in the ears like a cry. They went back into Logres, and at sight of new things and new places, Kigva's eyes brightened, as Manawyddan had hoped they would. She was too young to be always sad.

They found a town they liked, and they stopped there.

"Lord," said Kigva, "what craft will you take? Let it be one that is seemly, for I am still tired of being run out of town."

But for once Manawyddan was contrary; his own load of bitterness was too new and too heavy.

"I will take no craft but the one I had before. I will make shoes."

Kigva looked very straight at him then. As perhaps she had seen the witches look at Gwynn Gloyu.

"Lord, you know well that competing with boors always gets you into trouble. And shoemaking is no business for a man so nobly born as you."

"Well would it be," said Manawyddan, "if no highborn man ever did anything worse. I make shoes, and another man pays me for them, and if they are good shoes and fit him, where is the harm? Did Caswallon earn his throne as honorably—that throne that people are beginning to forget that Bran my brother ever held?"

Kigva said sternly, "We are not talking about Caswallon, who is a bad smell. We are talking about you."

"I will make shoes," said Manawyddan.

He made golden shoes as before, and once the work was begun, Kigva took Pryderi's place and helped him cheerfully enough.

"Though I know how it will turn out," said she.

The moons passed; they prospered. But before the year was quite up, Kigva began to notice that some of the townswomen were not as friendly to her as they had been. She spoke about it to Manawyddan.

"They are all shoemakers' wives or kin, Lord. It seems to me that it would be better if you did not make quite such good shoes."

He sighed. "That is a weakness that is on me, girl. What I do I must do as well as I can."

Kigva sighed too. "Well, enough wisdom is with you to call it a weakness. It is going to get us into trouble again."

That night Manawyddan awoke. The room was dark and still, the moonlight did not reach his bed. But he could see, quite plainly, a little brown bird sitting on his breast. He said, without surprise, "You are Branwen's bird. The starling she reared in the meal trough and sent to tell us how she, who had gone into Ireland a Queen, was now but a beaten slave."

The bird said, "That is so. And before you went to Ireland to deliver my Lady, you gave me into the keeping of another Queen. Of Rhiannon Oset of Faery."

Memory came to Manawyddan. "She told me that you had found a mate and flown away."

"Yes. She set me free to love my love and build my nest and rear my broods as a bird should. Until that dread night—the night of the storm that came upon Dyved from beyond the world. I died then, of the great sound; I who was no longer young."

"Then why did you not go back to Branwen?" Manawyddan asked, still without surprise.

"I did, and glad was our meeting. But for this one night she sends me back. For your sake, as once she sent me upon a long journey for her own. And this time I know the meaning of the words I speak. She says, '*Brother, beware.*'"

"Of what? Or of whom?"

"Of men who are losing their living because you outdo them at their own craft. Who will kill you if you are still here when the moon rises again."

"Well, that is not to be wondered at. Is that all her word?"

"No. She says that when you go back to Dyved—as well she knows that you will go back—you must still beware of—of—oh, I cannot speak the name! It clutches my throat like a hand, it weighs down my tongue like lead!" He felt how her tiny body trembled, even though no weight or substance of earth was in it any longer.

"Rest, little one," he said. "Be still. Perhaps I can help."

He spoke words of power then; words such as the wisest of High Druids seldom spoke but twice in a lifetime, and then only when they taught or were taught them, mystic mighty sounds to serve against that terrible uttermost need that most likely would never come. But his own tongue seemed to swell and harden until it was like a stone in his mouth. The sounds would not come clearly. Sweat stood on his forehead.

The night outside was quiet, but within that room a thin wind rose. It ruffled the starling's unearthly feathers; blew ice-cold through Manawyddan's hair.

"I must go," the bird whispered. "Back—to—her. There—even He cannot reach me."

"He?"

She set her beak against his ear. Soft as the sound of grass growing was her whisper now. "The Gray Man—the son of Him that Hides in the Wood—*Oh-h Oh-h! Beware—beware!*"

As a feather is swept away by a wind, so she was whirled away. But just before she vanished, Manawyddan saw a ray of moonlight strike her, enfold her like a shining mantle. Glad at heart, he thought, *Branwen has power to guard her messenger*. Then darkness took him, and he sank again into that mysterious healing gulf that men call sleep.

When he woke, the sun was high, and the good smell of food came to him; Kigva was cooking breakfast. For a breath's space he lay still, then remembered all and leapt up.

"Girl, we must be out of here before nightfall!"

Kigva dropped the spoon with which she was stirring their porridge, and it fell into the hot porridge, and splashed her, and made her jump. Then she said with some asperity, "Well, Lord, I told you so. But who else has told you?"

"A little bird."

Kigva looked at him sharply. "One with feathers?"

"It had feathers once."

Her face grew grave. "Not—one of the Birds of Rhiannon?"

"No. If they have found her, they stay with her. Make haste and pack now girl. There are things I must do."

"There certainly are things you ought to do, Lord—there are indeed. Why should we bear this from these boors?"

"Boors or not, they have a right to live. It is time for us to go home, girl. Back to Dyved."

"Home," said Kigva; and her face changed and softened. "Home!"

But that night, when they were tramping through the lonely woods, three laden donkeys with them (buying and loading those beasts had been Manawyddan's task), she grew curious again.

"What did give you warning this time, Lord? Have the winds begun to carry men's words to you, as they do to Mâth the Ancient?"

"Mâth hears men's thoughts, not their words, girl; and in this age that gift is his alone."

"Then have you taken to sleeping upon a bull's hide? I have never seen it when I made your bed."

"Child, no druid of the Old Tribes ever slept

upon a bull's hide. Only they of the New Tribes, that learned druidry from us, but still refuse to live by the Ancient Harmonies, ever needed such devices to focus the Eye within."

Kigva thought that over. "I have heard Pendaran Dyved say such things, Lord, and he talking with Rhiannon. But if things that cannot move of themselves truly have no power over men, why did all our ill luck come on us after Caswallon took away the Holy Stones?"

Manawyddan said slowly, "To us four the taking of the Stones made no difference. But to the people of Dyved—who knows? Generations of faith and worship may pour power into a thing even as sailors putting out to sea pour water—that may well mean life to them—into jug or cask. And when the Stones went, they of Dyved who so long had put their faith in them may not have had power enough left to withstand the fear that shook them out of life and time."

Kigva thought again, then shook her head. "Lord, I would like to say I see. But the truth is that I do not see at all."

They went on awhile, then she spoke again. "Lord, next year will be the seventh year since the Great Storm. Folk say that in the seventh year, and in it only, can Otherworldly spells be broken and all that has been taken away be brought back. Could all Dyved come back? Could—even *they* come back?"

Manawyddan knew who she meant by "they." He said gently, "Pray to the Mothers that it may be so, child. But do not set your hopes upon it."

She spoke no more that night.

Cold and lonely was that journey. Winter's teeth already were biting, frost-white, through the autumn winds. The trees that at first flamed like torches soon were stripped and bare, their naked boughs shivering in the gusts, the fallen leaves beneath them brown as themselves. All their brief glory of red and gold was gone, withered as their summer greenness. Soon man and girl wore their heavy cloaks even at midday, and when night came they tethered the donkeys where the trees grew lowest, and there was most shelter.

"This is not nice," Kigva said once, shivering as the wind's teeth sought to pierce her cloak. She drew the good wool closer around her.

"It will be worse," said Manawyddan, looking worriedly at the vast, darkening cloud masses above them, "if rain comes."

Before long rain did come. Cold and gray it beat upon them, soaked them through. It turned their sodden clothes from friends to foes; foes that clung clammily, implacably, to their chilled wet bodies. Mists hid all. Long before night came they were stumbling, squishing blindly through unseen, clawing entanglements of branch and briar. When night came the blackness was utter; they could not light a fire. If Manawyddan's long, patient labor did raise a spark from the damp faggots they gathered, the black, savage downpour beat it out.

They went on unrested, unwarmed by food or drink. The next day was the same, and the next night.

On the third day the ground became more stony, ceased to suck at their wet feet.

"This is better," said Kigva hopefully. "We can move more quickly now. Get somewhere sooner."

By "somewhere," she meant a house with a roof over it and a fire inside it. Manawyddan, who knew that in that drenched, darkened world they might already have passed near many such pleasant places, had the heart to answer only, "Maybe."

The ground grew stonier; sloped steadily upward. Soon they knew that they must be on a hillside. The wind slashed at them more fiercely, the climbing put fresh strain upon their tired legs. But Manawyddan's eyes lit up, and he peered forward, through that blinding, beating sheet of rain.

"These must be the hills of the Preseli," he said. "I thought that we should be getting near them. Near home."

The Preseli, thought Kigva, where the Stones were. And she remembered how different everything had been when the Stones were in their ancient places; all the light and laughter and warmth at Arberth, and Pryderi joking and scuffling with her in the daytime, and lying lovingly beside her at night.

She plodded on quietly, but now the wetness of her face was no longer cold; it was hot and salty. It rolled slowly down her cheeks, beneath the rain that still beat upon them.

Night was falling when at last they saw the walls of a house. They ran toward it, their hearts leaping with gladness, yet full of fear too. What if this longed-for refuge should turn out to be only a wish-shape, something that would vanish in the mist?

It did not. It was solid. Its doorway loomed dark and still as night, yet to them seemed warm and welcoming as a firelit hearth. They rushed in, and Kigva dropped down, spent and gasping, giving up at last. Manawyddan groped until he found the fireplace; there was wood in it. Soon the fire blazed up and he saw the bare walls around them; saw the pots and pans and scanty furniture, the long-unused bed-place. Saw and caught his breath.

This was the shepherd's hut where he and Pryderi had guested on that long-gone night before they came to Arberth. Everything was just as it had been then. Only the old shepherd and his wife were gone.

In a chest were blankets, dry and clean. On a hook hung the old woman's cloak, as free of dust as if she had just washed and dried it. Manawyddan brought it and one of the blankets to Kigva.

"Get out of those wet things as fast as you can, child: you are soaked. I will take another blanket."

Kigva reeled to her feet. "I will start supper first, Lord. Do you change now; you have done enough, starting the fire by yourself."

"It was no trouble; these logs are dry."

"It will take only a minute to start supper." Kigva's jaw was set, though her teeth chattered a little.

"It will take longer than that. First we must bring out food and unpack it . . ."

"Because it is on the donkeys. Help me bring them in."

And Manawyddan helped her, because he did not want to lay hands on her, and there was no other way of stopping her. While she cooked and the donkeys huddled as close to the fire as she would let them, their shaggy hides dripping, he went to the bed-place and at last began to take his wet clothes off. The blessed warmth of a dry blanket was just closing around his tired, soaked body when he heard a thin, nastily delighted cackle of laughter behind him.

"It is not much fear you are able to put on your woman, Man of the Big People."

Manawyddan spun around. Deep in the deepest shadows he saw something.

Brown knees were there, and a small brown face gnarled as old wood, and the biggest mouth he had ever seen on anything, with the laughter still coming out of it, between whiskers that were as gray as cobwebs and as dirty.

There was great originality in those whiskers, for they grew upward instead of downward, and out of their owner's ears and eyebrows as well as his cheeks and chin.

"Indeed," said Manawyddan, "you must be a bogey."

"Indeed I am," said the bogey, "and it is glad I am to see anybody, even you and that pert chit of a girl, to whom something will soon happen if those miserable donkeys she would drag in dirty up my nice clean house. It has been a long time since I have had anybody to plague. A very long time." And he sighed.

"I am sorry for that," said Manawyddan courteously, "though if you try to plague either of us you will soon be sorrier. But I should have known you were here. This house does not look like a house that has been deserted for years."

"It does not indeed," said the bogey with pride. "You would think the shepherd's wife had just stepped out. She used to say that she did not see how she could ever have got along without me, and since she always put out a bowl of fresh milk and the best of everything for me, I never let her find out. Indeed, since she has been gone I have found out that she could manage to do a few things by herself."

"I do not doubt that," said Manawyddan.

"It is true, though I would never admit it if I got her back. Women should never be allowed to get above themselves. Like that one of yours, who would bring in those donkeys."

"She did well," said Manawyddan. "They are cold and wet."

"If they do what I am afraid they will do I will rub her face in it. We bogeys have our rights. We can make the work of a house go as smooth and easy as pouring cream out of a jug, or as full of accidents and mishaps as a fishnet is of holes. There is nobody like us."

"There will soon be nobody like you here if you try to play tricks on Kigva." Manawyddan said quietly.

"None of you clumsy Big People could ever get a hand on me," said the bogey comfortably. "I will be here long after both of you are gone."

"Maybe. But I or any other druid-bred man could put an awl through your nose and raise a wind that would blow you away to be spun through the upper air above the eastern seas for the length of twice seven generations."*

For the first time the bogey met his eyes squarely; those sea-gray eyes of the son of Llyr. He squirmed.

"Do not do that," he begged. "It was done to a cousin of mine, and he is not back yet. His mother is afraid that when he does get back he will have rheumatism forever. Those upper winds are cold—nobody knows quite how cold." He shivered. "I did not dream you were a man of knowledge, Lord; seeing how foolishly easy you are on the girl."

"You know it now, Remember it."

"I wish I did not have to. But truly it is good to have people here again. I am so glad to see you that there will not be a single lump in the girl's porridge tonight; though that will not be easy to manage, for it is plain that the little fool never has been taught how to make porridge. Or anything else."

To that Manawyddan had no answer. Little things can be vexing as well as great ones, and often, since he lost Rhiannon, he had been ashamed to think how glad he would have been if the Nine Witches had taught Kigva how to cook. Rhiannon evidently had found it easier and more tactful to use her own magic on the food than to teach a grown daughter-in-law.

Kigva called, "Supper will soon be ready, Lord. If you will come and watch it, I can change now."

*For the disciplining of an objectionable household bogey see John Rhys's *Celtic Folklore*, vol. II.

"She cannot hear my voice," the bogey said composedly. "Not unless I want her to. And I do not want her to. She is not a person with whom one could carry on an intelligent conversation."

"Any conversation between you and her would soon become a quarrel," said Manawyddan, "so none had better start." To Kigva he called, "I am coming girl. You should have changed long ago."

13

The Warning and the Sowing

Toward morning Manawyddan woke, or seemed to wake. He saw the little house about him, gray and still. Then of a sudden that grayness grew, widened and expanded, into infinite space; into depths terrible and unknowable, through which Eyes watched him. He heard a Voice that made no sound say clearly: *"Here we first met, mortal, your eyes and Mine. Turn back now lest we meet once again, and for the last time. For no man may dwell in Dyved, that by My will must be a wilderness forever."*

Manawyddan started up. But now, in the fading darkness that was still more black than gray, the house was small and snug around him. He heard Kigva's quiet breathing, and remembered how, on that other night, when it was Pryderi who lay near him in the dark, he had faced in dream or vision that danger that then as now he could not remember, yet knew to be terribly real. *"Why do You veil Yourself from my waking mind, Enemy? Would You turn me back or drive me on?"*

Beside him came again the bogey's cackling laughter. "So there is Something that has power to put fear on you too, O Man of Illusion and Fantasy."

Manawyddan said, "What did you see, imp?"

"Only you. You and that girl, who at least does not snore. But I saw you jump, Lord."

Manawyddan said more slowly, "What did you see on the night of the Great Storm? When Dyved was laid waste?"

The bogey shivered. "Not much, Lord. Yet too much. The shepherd and his wife were already sound asleep. They might not have been, at that time of night, had they been younger. I can remember lively times in this sleeping-place." He chuckled. "Age draws the heat out of men and women, Lord. Mere tiredness took it out of you and the girl last night."

"My stepson is her man, not I."

The bogey cackled once more. "Your stepson! You never had one. Only Big People would have been big enough fools to swallow that tale, Lord. I know who you are now; we bogeys too have our ways of coming at knowledge, and last night I used them." He sobered, looking puzzled. "But Pryderi has been gone a long time. Why isn't his woman your woman now?"

"Because she still loves him. And I am neither young enough nor old enough to want to sleep with young girls."

"Well," said the bogey, "these giggling, ticklish girls can be a nuisance in a sensible man's bed. They have not even got sense enough to stop talking and let a man sleep when he has had enough and wants to rest. They are forever wagging their heads off, and it is not that end of them that is interesting at all."

"They are not the only tongue-waggers. I asked

you what happened on the night of the Great Storm."

The bogey shivered again. "I would rather wag my tongue about anything else. I never think about that night. I have forgotten as much about it as I could."

"Yet this once remember all you can. Tell me all you can. I will not ask it of you again."

"Well, as I said, Lord, the old couple slept. And my work was done, so I listened to them snore, as I had many another night. They did not do it in tune, and sometimes one of them did it louder than the other, and all those snorts and wheezes and rumbles were very interesting to listen to. More entertaining than the noises the old folk made when they were awake."

"You still play with words. Get to the point."

"I am doing what you asked, Lord; telling you everything I can remember. That was a night like many other nights. And then the thunder came." He paused, and this time Manawyddan waited, and did not hurry him.

"The thunder came, and then the rain, and the great winds." The bogey shuddered. "There are always riders on the winds, but that night there were many, many. Not your ordinary human dead, that look down with regret and longing or else with forgiving friendliness—maybe even a little wink—upon this earth that once they walked. There was no regret in these, and no friendliness. Only power; power, and the will to destroy. I was afraid." Again he stopped, his teeth chattering.

"What did they look like, those riders?" urged Manawyddan. "Tell me."

"I cannot. They can be seen only as graynesses and whirlings; they whirl and whirl, and have no shape. In their own world they must wear forms, but in ours they have none. But they were terrible, and they came.

"The whole house rocked and shook, as if they were trying to tear it off the earth, and hurl it out into the night beyond the world. I crouched in my corner and shook; I shook like a leaf in that mighty wind; and the shepherd and his wife woke and shook also. Once she screamed, but in that din the sound was little, no more than the rustling of a leaf. After that she and the old man only clung together, burrowing into each other's warmth. But still they shook.

"We all three shook, so that it was a pain, a wrenching, jerking pain tearing at the very us inside us. An agony that could end only with our ending, with the very shaking of ourselves into bits. Not while one toe or finger held together, not while one hair grew beside another, could we know peace.

"We shook, the shepherd and his old woman and I, we shook . . .

"Had I been as solid as they were I would have come apart as they did. I saw their bodies wink and waver like torch flames, and finally go out. I saw where they had been, for they were not . . .

"And after that I did not know much, I did not feel or think much, for a long time.

"In the morning, when everything was quiet and golden again, and I was still sitting here, stunned and dizzy, two dragonflies flew into the house. They looked all around, they settled here and there, and then flew away again. But I knew them.

"Sometimes they used to come back, often at first. I could tell which was the woman by the way she hovered over her possessions, and sometimes lit on them and felt them with her feelers, as if loving them and remembering. But that was all she could do, and in time I grew tired of it, and of their queer fluttery ways, and began chasing them out whenever they flew in."

"That was very cruel of you," said Manawyddan.

"It was very bogeyish," said the bogey.

Toward sunset Manawyddan and Kigva and the donkeys came to Arberth. And never had Manawyddan been better pleased than when he saw his home again, and the green lands where he had walked with Rhiannon and Pryderi. Never before had he realized how fully it had become home, this house where his son had been born, though he had not.

Even to see Harlech again would not be like this. Harlech was my home because it was Bran's home; there I laughed and worked with my brother and helped him—or thought I helped him—to build peace and happiness for the world we knew. To weld Old Tribes and New into one people. But here I lived with Rhiannon; here in our youth and her ignorance we joyously begot our son; here in our ripeness and in our knowledge we loved. We too laughed and built and worked together; for ourselves and for those who would come after us; some of them of our own blood. Now has all that too come to nothing?

His mind said yes; all the quiet ruin around him said it. Yet in his heart the foolish-seeming gladness would not die.

Kigva, watching his face, braced herself and thought sturdily, *He is getting old. I have acted like a little girl, making him bear my tears and my fears and my loss, that is no greater than his. From now on I must be strong. Let him sit and dream; his time for that is coming, and he has earned it.*

And she thought with wonder that she loved him better than she ever had her own father Gwynn Gloyu, that great, swaggering warrior who had tried so hard to be a man in spite of the Nine Witches, and never had quite brought it off . . .

Somehow the great lonely halls of Arberth seemed to have a quiet friendliness about them that night; not the chill and crying emptiness the homecomers had feared. And when she and Manawyddan had unloaded the donkeys and made them comfortable, Kigva set herself to cook the best supper that she ever had cooked. She succeeded: both to her surprise and Manawyddan's it was as good as any that Rhiannon had ever set before them. Not until later, when she had gone to bed, did the son of Llyr find out why.

He was sitting alone beside the fire when in the shadows something moved. He started, then relaxed. *Good would be any ghost that came here. Perhaps it is my wife; or my boy.*

It came nearer, out of the shadows, into the light. Something more solid than memory; something small and brown and gnarled.

"I am here," said the bogey.

"So I see," said Manawyddan. "But I thought you bogeyfolk never left a house unless ill-treatment was put upon you there. And in the shepherd's hut none was. Before we left, Kigva and I cleaned up the mess that I will admit the donkeys made."

The bogey looked embarrassed. "It is our custom, Lord, as you say, never to leave the house we have chosen until some fool offends us. But this I will say: I was old before the oldest oak in Dyved was an acorn, yet all those years before did not seem so long as the few I have spent in that hut since the shepherd and his wife blew away. Clumsy and stupid and ill-tempered as you Big People are, one gets bored without you. I would like to come and haunt your house."

Manawyddan stroked his chin. "That could have both advantages and disadvantages," he said.

"What disadvantages? Did that fool of a girl ever cook you such a supper before? Nothing you eat will ever be underdone or overdone or anything but good—very good—so long as I am with you."

Manawyddan stroked his chin again. "And Kigva? How will it be for her?"

The bogey looked at him imploringly. "I will not play many tricks on her, Lord. Just enough to keep my hand in. If she treats me with proper respect, nobody could be nicer to her than I will be. Most of the time, anyway."

"All of the time," said Manawyddan, "if you stay here."

The bogey drew himself up with great dignity; he looked all of three feet tall, "Lord, it is custom

too for a bowl of milk and bread to be set out
every night for a bogey. If she is careless—if the
milk has begun to sour, or the bread is just a wee
bit stale—then she must pay. That too is a bogey's
right; worth even freezing in the upper air for."

"I think you had better go home," said
Manawyddan.

"Lord, I would not scald her in any place where
it would show! I might trip her up now and then,
but I would not break an arm or leg on her—that I
swear. By the sun and the moon, and by the oath
that bogies swear by."

"Bogey, I thank you for a good dinner, but my
daughter and I can manage by ourselves. Goodbye."

"Are you sure, Lord? That girl is so clumsy that
she could have worse accidents by herself than I
would ever arrange for her. She likes and understands nothing about a kitchen, and nothing in a
kitchen likes or understands her."

"Are you threatening us?" Manawyddan's voice
was suddenly silken-soft. All the bogey's whiskers
stood up in alarm.

"No, Lord. Into many houses I could enter unseen and make mischief, but here I dare not risk
it. A man of knowledge like you would find me
out. But consider—think of the meals you had
yesterday and today, and of all the ones you had
before. And a young woman gets above herself
when all goes well and she thinks that she is doing
it all herself—she needs a lesson. And both in the
kitchen and out of it she is the better for having
learned one. Think of your comfort and of the
girl's own good, Lord. I will do her no real harm."

Manawyddan said, "I myself will prepare and set out your bowl each evening, and if you have any objections to what is in it, we will fight them out together. But raise one burn or one bruise on Kigva, and I will blow you away into the upper air for three times seven generations. That I swear by the sun and the moon, and by the oath my people swear by."

The bogey brightened. "Lord, I will watch over her as if she were the tenderest of lamb roasts."

And so he did. From that day on, no man and woman could have fared better than Manawyddan and Kigva did. When he hunted and brought home game, the meat never burned, and if Kigva gathered herbs that were too green, they somehow ripened in the pot. And when she did her washing, the dirt came out as easily as if it had only been perching like a bird on the top of the cloth, and never had got down into it at all.

Kigva always had been one for losing things too, but now she could find whatever she wanted at once, even when she could have sworn that she never had put it in the place where it suddenly appeared under her nose.

All this good luck and easy living began to get on her nerves. She tried to think that Rhiannon was watching over her and helping her, but the Presence that she sometimes felt near her did not seem at all like Rhiannon's.

Then one night on her way to bed she remembered she had forgotten something and turned back to the kitchen to see to it. She saw Manawyddan setting out the bowl of milk and bread, and understood.

"Lord, there is a bogey in this house!"

"Let there be no fright on you for that, girl," said Manawyddan placidly. "He does no harm. He only helps."

"There is no fright on me," said Kigva. "Is the niece of Nine Witches to be frightened of a little mite of a bogey? But indeed—" and as she thought things over her face lengthened until it became very long indeed, "this does explain things. Too many things."

After that she was more nervous than ever, and the bogey complained to Manawyddan. "It is even harder than it was to keep her from having accidents, Lord. I never saw such a girl for doing things wrong."

Kigva complained too. "It is hard on me always to be wondering where he is. Whether he is in front of me or behind me, or on which side of me he is. To know that he is watching me, and that whatever I do I cannot get away from him. And I always feel that he is laughing at me, Lord."

"I am not," said the bogey, who was still there. "She makes me too much work for that."

"Can you not feel grateful for his help?" said Manawyddan.

"He is very useful," said Kigva, "and indeed I wish he were a bother. I wish now that I had let my aunts teach me magic, as they wished to do. But witches always use black magic; they sing a great many incantations over a great many bubbling cauldrons full of queer things. I never felt that I could bear to memorize all those rigmaroles and then sing them in the middle of such a bad smell. But if I had . . ."

"He does not stay with you except when you are at work," said Manawyddan comfortingly. "He and I understand each other. There is no need for you to worry your head about him."

"What head she has," said the bogey, grinning.

The bogey was a great help to Kigva, but he was also an insult. She could no longer take pride in her own handiwork, knowing how much of it was likely to be his, and to have too little pride is as unhealthy for either man or woman as it is to have too much. Manawyddan saw her trouble and pitied it but he did not know what to do. His bargain with the bogey was made, and he pitied the gnome's loneliness too.

Winter howled over the land. Ice covered the rivers, snow whitened the brown earth and made shining lacy beauty of the leafless trees. Winds beat against the palace walls; sharp as knives, stronger than the arms of men, they tore at the thatched roof. Manawyddan had to climb up to mend it, and the bogey went along to help him. Kigva burned a batch of bread in the kitchen, and clapped her hands for joy.

Now if I work fast I can make and bake the next batch by myself. O Mothers, let it be good!

It was. That night, when at last the tired Manawyddan was safe back in the warm hall, she served it proudly and he complimented her upon it. Her face shone like the long-gone summer sun.

"Indeed, Lord, now you see that it was a good thing to have that bogey up there with you, keeping you from breaking a leg on that slippery roof, and not bothering me in my nice kitchen!"

The bogey snorted, and Manawyddan said "Shh!" But the light in her face did not die.

In his weariness, Manawyddan even let her fill the bogey's bowl that night, though he cautioned her sternly to taste everything herself and be sure that it was of the best. She did so, but when she set out the bowl and a generous helping of her new-made bread with it, she said proudly, "Sure I am that you never have tasted better, bogey. Remember well now that you had no hand in the making of it. It is not I who ever needed you or asked you here, but the Lord Manawyddan. Though of course you are welcome, being his guest."

"It was fairly decent bread," the bogey told Manawyddan later. "Which was as well for her, in spite of you, Lord."

"Remember our bargain," said Manawyddan drowsily.

"I do. Otherwise I would have tweaked that turned-up nose of hers for her, Lord. I nearly did anyhow."

"I am glad you did not. The upper winds would be especially cold now, little friend."

The bogey said, "I know it. Still, that girl of yours had better watch her tongue, or tomorrow or the day after she may take a bite of something while it is still too hot."

But Manawyddan looked at him then, and for the rest of that evening the bogey was only two feet tall. His height varied according to his mood; sometimes he was three feet tall and sometimes less, for bogeys do not belong to so solid a crust of the universe as the world we know.

Spring came at last. Ice and snow melted; under the brown bark of the trees and under the brown breast of the Mother a multitude of tiny lives stirred; they that rise up to make all greenness, leaves and grass and moss.

Manawyddan took the last load of grain, the one he had saved for seed. He chose three fields, he ploughed and he planted. The bogey went with him and helped him, so once more Kigva had peace in her kitchen. Sometimes things went wrong, but often they went right. She was learning; given time, her hurt pride, her desire to show that she could do things well by herself, would make an excellent cook of her.

Summer came, with her arms full of flowers; that most ancient bride who is ever honey-sweet, ever-young; she that rises in ever-renewed maidenhood to be clasped in the arms of the Young God, Her deliverer. He whose warm winds stir Her to inexhaustible and joyous motherhood.

She came, and the wheat in the three fields sprang up. The *Mabinogi* says that no wheat in the world ever sprang up better.

The bogey looked at it and not only grew three feet tall, but stayed that way. He said to himself, *This is the fruit of my help.*

Manawyddan and Kigva looked, and were happy. She said, "Next winter we will have plenty of meal, Lord."

There had been a little time, when the meal had grown low and what grain was left had to be saved for seed, when the ice still covered the fish, and it was not safe to track game far in the snowy woods, when they had been hungry. Not hungry enough to make them afraid, but hungrier than people like to be.

Manawyddan smiled and said, "No. Next winter there will be no need to tighten our belts."

No doubt he did not fear the ordinary hazards of weather as an ordinary farmer must; his druid power could keep them off. Yet he does seem to have been overconfident; the glamour was falling over his eyes again, that same glamour that for seven years now had fallen so easily upon any eyes in Dyved, that Land of Illusion. He of all men should have remembered that the Enemy might still be watching, playing with them as a cat plays with mice.

The summer wore; harvest time drew near. Manawyddan went to look at the field he had first planted, and saw it was ripe. "Tomorrow I will reap it," he said.

"Why not now?" said the bogey beside him.

"Because the sun is already high. Before I had finished I would be as wet as the sealfolk that dwell in the sea."

"Not with me to help you, Lord."

"Maybe not, and my thanks be with you, but the crop will only be the better for one more day's ripening."

Manawyddan, too, like Kigva, did not feel that it would be wise to become too dependent on the bogey.

He went home and told Kigva, and she rejoiced and cooked a fine supper. Once, when a pitcher of milk upset and then seemed suddenly to steady itself in midair, and then sailed quietly back through that air to land quietly on the table, she even smiled and said, "Thank you, bogey."

They ate and slept, but the blackness of night had hardly begun to pale before the oncoming tread of morning's bright feet when Manawyddan rose. He breakfasted, and set out.

He saw the stars twinkle and go out, vanishing into the grayness like golden jewels snatched away by unseen mighty hands. He felt the dew upon his face, like heavy tears except that it was cold.

He walked under a gray heaven, through a gray land, for as yet the dawn was not strong enough for color, that eldest child of light, to be reborn. He thought suddenly, coldly, *Grayness, grayness*— Like a bird, the half memory hovered above his head in that pale darkness, then flew away and was gone.

He came to the field; and he stopped stock-still. For nothing but ruin was there. All was trampled and crushed as if by a herd of great beasts. He went through the field from end to end, and saw that not only was every stalk trampled flat, but that every ear of wheat had been cut from each stalk, as cleanly as with a knife, and that each ear was gone.

Nothing but straw was left.

He went to look at the second field, and every stalk in it stood upright, straight as a young warrior or a young tree. Tall and golden, and heavy with ears of the finest wheat. He stood and looked at it long, his gray eyes narrowed. Then, I will reap this one tomorrow, he told himself.

"Why tomorrow? We will reap it today!" Kigva raged, when he came home and told her what had happened. "I will go with you and help! So will the bogey: we will get this crop in before anything can happen to it."

"Tomorrow we will reap it," said Manawyddan.

Kigva looked at him with wonder. "Lord, what is on you? It is not yourself that is acting like this."

"Tomorrow we will reap the field," said Manawyddan.

That night supper was not so good. When Kigva upset something, the bogey forgot to catch it. It went all over her feet, and she did not like that, because it was hot. She was very angry, and used language that she had learned from the Nine Witches.

For the first time the bogey appeared before her.

"Lady," he said, "I did not do that on purpose. It was only your own clumsiness. If you will promise not to tell the Lord Manawyddan what has happened, I will do a little charm that will unburn your feet at once."

"Do it then," said Kigva, "and I will not."

He did it, and she felt of her feet wonderingly, finding the skin as white and smooth as ever. Then she said curiously to the bogey, "Why are you afraid of the Lord Manawyddan? He is the kindest of men."

"He could blow me away onto the upper winds, Lady."

"He has not got sense enough left to do any such thing," said Kigva. "But if you let me spill anything more, I will tell him and see what he can do. For we cannot afford to waste any more food.

It is in my mind that we are going to be starved out of Dyved this time. And if we try to live any-where else we never last long." And she sighed.

"You may not last long if you stay here," said the bogey. "For something is happening again, and every time something has happened before, somebody has vanished. And this time there is no-body left to vanish but you and the Lord Mana-wyddan. I shall be sorry to see him go, even if he is unreasonable at times." And he sighed too.

"Vanish yourself," said Kigva, and threw a pot at him. He did, into thin air, and she went to bed, but not to sleep. For long she tossed, restless and miserable and afraid, and then suddenly the sun was shining in her eyes. It was bright day, but when she rose she found that she was alone in the palace. Manawyddan was gone. So was the bogey, for the kitchen had the feeling of a dead place that can have no life in it, seen or unseen.

She sat down then and wept. And sobbing, thought, *I would not mind vanishing if I would be with you again, Pryderi. Whatever kind of place we were in, I could be happy there with you. At least a little happy. But what if we were not together? What if vanishing means being alone in the cold and the dark? Or even*—her teeth chattered—*being nowhere?*

In the gray of dawn Manawyddan had come to the second field. Had looked at it and seen that it was ruined as the other. Nothing but trampled straw and trampled stalks were left. Not one ear of corn remained; only the useless, earless straw.

He looked and he raised his arms above his

head and shook his clenched fists at the heavens. "Woe!" he cried. "O gracious Mothers, who is my destroyer? But I know well who He is: He that sought my ruin from the beginning is completing it, and He has destroyed the whole country along with me!"

Then he strode away as fast as his legs would carry him. He came to the third field, the last that was left, and now the young sun was coming up, and under her tender rays it shone like a whole field of gold, as beautiful as any wheat that ever grew. He looked at it, and his jaw set.

"Shame upon me," he said, "if I do not watch here tonight! Whatever robbed the other fields will come back to rob this field, and I shall see what it is."

But when he went home and told Kigva his plan, she raged again. "Lord, has all the wisdom gone out of you? You that were once so wise?"

But her words did not trouble him, any more than if she had been a sea gull beating her wings against a cliff.

"I will watch the field tonight," he said. And he got out his spear, and all his other arms, and set to work polishing them. "I will be ready for whoever comes."

"Pryderi was armed," said Kigva, near to tears. "Armed he went into that place he never came out of. Rhiannon had her magic, yet she too never came back. Whatever will come tonight is strong— too strong for any power known to men."

"I ploughed those fields and sowed them, girl; I put my strength and my sweat into them. I will not be robbed without a fight." Manawyddan's jaw was still set; the look in his gray eyes was not his own.

Kigva wept aloud. "Will you leave me here all alone, Lord? The only human being left in this whole land? What shall I do? How shall I live?"

"I will watch the field tonight."

Kigva's sobs ceased. She said quietly, "Lord, I see that your own good mind has left you, and that whatever Spider caught the others has you in His web. Well, I will go get you a good supper; it will be your last."

She went to the kitchen, and called softly into the air, "Bogey, give me something to put in his food—to make him sleep here through that third field's ruin. This blow at least I will try to stop."

Above her the bogey laughed. "Girl, you are wiser than I thought!" For the second and last time she saw him, swinging comfortably among the rafters.

But that night it was she who slept soundly; so soundly that she never heard Manawyddan rise and leave the house.

14

The Gray Man Comes

Before moonrise Manawyddan came to the field. He sat down under a tree close beside it, and waited. He saw the sky darken and the stars come out, that myriad shining host that each night keeps watch over the earth and perhaps prevents even darker deeds than do happen in the darkness. He saw the moon come up, queenly and proud among them, her cheeks flushed with the red-gold of harvest time.

He heard the sleepy twittering of the birds, and the silence that followed it. He heard an owl hoot somewhere in the woods. He saw the dark shadow of the Mound of Arberth loom black through the blackness, with a darkness so deep that it seemed no light ever could reach or pierce it forever. That Mound whose black side had closed upon the two he had loved best on earth . . .

He sat there and waited. The night wore.

"It is getting late," said the bogey.

Manawyddan looked around and saw him crouching among the gnarled roots of the tree. He was small; he was very small; smaller than the son of Llyr had ever seen him.

"You here! Where is Kigva?"

"Safe at home," said the bogey. "She cannot

182

follow us or worry. I drugged her as you bade me, though I still think hers was the better plan. I do not know what made me foolish enough to come with you myself."

"You were indeed a fool. Your being is too light and small to face What will come here tonight. Go—go before you get yourself blown away, not for twice seven aeons, but forever."

"I would," said the bogey, "if I dared." He shivered. "Whatever is coming is already on Its way. I can feel that, though I cannot tell from which direction It is coming. Maybe It is vast enough to come from all ways at once."

"Then lie still; maybe you can escape Its notice. Do nothing, for you cannot help me."

"You cannot help yourself either," said the bogey.

"I can try. That is what men are sent to earth for: to learn and to try."

The bogey made no answer. They listened hard, but they heard nothing but the silence; silence that is always a web of a myriad of tiny, interlacing sounds. Their own breathing became strands in that web; part of its dreadful, waiting quiet.

But nothing happened. Not one footfall out of all those pattering clawed softnesses came near them. Not one sound took on size or purpose; any purpose that had to do with them . . .

The moon rose higher. The night wore. Midnight came.

It happened then. That terrible, blazing spear of light shot out, stretching from end to end of heaven, slashing across the moon's bright face. All the stars of heaven seemed to be falling, and as they fell, the sky roared with thunder. Earth herself seemed to shake beneath the force of that blast that was the loudest ever heard.

When Manawyddan and the bogey took their hands from their ears, when their stunned eyes saw again, the stars were landing. Each of that bright swarm, as it struck the earth, lost its radiance and became a mouse. And each of that numberless host of mice sprang light-swift for a stalk of wheat and ran up it. So many were they that the tall stalks bent beneath their weight as if before a great wind and crashed to earth. Then, still light-swift, each mouse fled away, a golden ear between his white, shining teeth.

With a cry of rage Manawyddan leapt among them. He beat at them with his spear, he stamped with his feet, but they ran across his feet and leapt over his spear. He could not touch them, he could not reach them, any more than if they had been birds flying through the sky. He tried to fix his eyes upon one single one of them, hoping that so he might make his aim true, but he could not, any more than if they had been a swarm of flying gnats. But he kept on trying; not again, as in that first mad rush, would he let panic overwhelm him.

Was one going a little slower than the others? The least, least bit slower? No faster than the fastest horse might race? He prayed that it was; prayed that hope might not blind his eyes as the glamour did.

It was going slower—if the swiftness of the fleetest hound or horse could be called slow. Its dark round sides were plump; almost misshapen. Being fatter than the others, it found the great golden ear of wheat harder to carry.

Like a hound himself, Manawyddan raced after it. Again and again he thought he had it. Twice he fell, when it was just a bare inch beyond his outspread fingers. Always it managed to keep just out of his reach.

They were nearing the field's edge. Soon the bushes and tall grasses would hide it.

He was gaining. It was a mere yard ahead of him. A foot ahead. An inch. He put forth all his speed. His heart seemed to be battering against the walls of his chest, as in the besiegers' hands a log batters the gates of a fortress. His strained muscles seemed to be tearing with each leap, each bound.

Not an inch ahead now. Not half an inch. Though the bushes, too, were not the length of his foot away.

With a gasping cry of triumph he pounced. And fell, his thwarted hands clutching the grasses: empty of all else.

But in his despair he heard another cry of triumph; shrill and small, but no mouse squeak. A voice he knew. It changed, even as he heard it, to a sharp cry of pain.

Manawyddan wrenched apart the grasses before him. He saw the bogey grasping the mouse, whose sharp white teeth, already sunk in his shoulder, were ready, as soon as its squirming body could wriggle a little higher, to close in his throat.

Manawyddan's iron fingers tore it away: gasped with pain himself as those sharp teeth met in the

flesh of his palm. The bogey sprang forward.
"Quick! Put her in this!"

The son of Llyr stared. He saw a glove of his
own, and a piece of string with it. But in the same
breath's space he was struggling to thrust his prey
into the dark opening of the glove. He and the
bogey between them could hardly get their tiny,
squirming captive inside, hardly make the cord
fast in time to keep it from wriggling out again.

When the deed was done they looked around,
panting, more than half expecting to go down
beneath a million sharp, fierce mice teeth.

But all was quiet in the moonlight. No living
thing was left among the bare straw that littered
that lovely field. Every mouse, like every ear of
wheat was gone. For awhile they stared in wonder. Then Manawyddan said quietly, "Force is not
their weapon."

"They have got enough of it for me." The bogey rubbed his shoulder. "Both of us together
could not have held her if I had not brought that
glove."

"How did you happen to bring it?"

"I had just followed you out of the house, Lord,
when I turned back to fetch it. A little bird flew
low over my head and told me to."

For a breath's space Manawyddan was silent.
"So? Well, I thank you, little friend; for that, and
for brave and loyal friendship." Under his breath
he said softly, "You too I thank, Branwen."

For another breath's space he seemed to meet
her eyes, dark and shining, glad as they had been
in childhood when she thought that she had
helped her brother to win some game. And he had

always let her think so, whether it was true or not.

And this time it was true, beloved, whether it is yourself or my memories that I see.

The bogey said, "I would not have come at all if I had known what I was getting into."

"But you did come," said Manawyddan.

Silently they went back to the palace together. In the hall they found Kigva, asleep before the fire. She sprang up, her eyes still dazed from the drug, but when they saw Manawyddan they became two lights.

"You are back, Lord! Safe!"

"I am, girl." Manawyddan went over to a peg on the wall, and hung the glove upon it. "We have lost our last field of wheat, but I have caught one of the robbers. Tomorrow I will hang her, and by the sun and the moon, if I had them, I would hang them all!"

Kigva stared. "Lord, what kind of robber could you get inside a glove?"

He told her then of the plague of mice and of the capture, and her face grew troubled.

"I would not want you to let it loose inside here, Lord—there is no love lost between the race of women and the race of mice—but why not let it loose outside? It is beneath a big man like you to hang a miserable little mouse."

"Girl, I would hang them all if I could catch them, and this mouse I will hang."

Kigva shrugged. She was feeling ashamed of her earlier fears; mice seemed unlikely allies for the Power who had laid all Dyved waste. The loss of the crops was a bitter blow, and the old man was taking it hard. Better to humor him.

"Well, Lord," she said, "do as you please."

They went to bed then. When Manawyddan rose the dawn was not gray, but flame-red and flame-gold.

He took down the glove, and felt one quick spasmodic jerk inside it. After that his prisoner lay still.

From the firewood he took sticks with which to build a doll-sized scaffold. He put them and the glove into a bag and with it over his shoulder he left the palace and the sleeping Kigva, and started for the Mound of Arberth.

Dark it loomed before him there in the rising sun, a grim stronghold of old night that the powers of day could never truly vanquish, and even the rays of light that touched its summit looked like a crown of all-devouring fire.

Manawyddan set foot upon its slope, and the bogey appeared beside him.

"Do you think this is wise, Lord?"

"Maybe so, maybe not. We will see."

"I do not want to see. Why challenge the Enemy here, on His own ground?"

"Little one, if force were His weapon He would have struck us all down long ago. It took Him years to entrap Rhiannon and Pryderi. It is by terror and by magic that He kills."

"And this is the best place for Him to do it, this Mound that is the entrance to the Underworld. Turn back, Lord, while you can! Let Him come after His mouse if He wants her."

"Another day in our world might be her death; I do not know the laws of her being. And only here, I am sure, can He show Himself by day."

"Well, good luck be with you!" said the bogey. "I am not brave enough to go with you this time." And he turned and trotted back down the mountainside.

Manawyddan went on. He knew that now indeed he was utterly alone; beyond all help from creatures of earth or even the loving dead. He had only himself to rely on now, and he knew that beside the powers of the Adversary any arts he knew were like a child's toys against the weapons of a man.

He came to the top of the Gorsedd; he came to its highest part. And there, with the red light beating down upon him, he set up two sticks. Only the crossbeam was needed to make a gallows. As he reached for the third stick he stopped stockstill, and his hand dropped at his side.

A bard was coming toward him; not a true bard but a singer of the lower rank, an old man in old, threadbare clothes. The man smiled at him and tried to meet his eyes, and Manawyddan suddenly knew that it would not be good to look long into those eyes. They were deep and strange, and as gray as his own.

"Lord," said the stranger, "Good day to you."

"The same to you, and my greeting, singer. But where have you come from?"

The stranger went on smiling; his eyes were still trying to catch Manawyddan's. "I have been singing these many moons in Lloegyr, Lord. Why do you ask?"

"Because for seven years I have seen no human beings in this land but four of my own family, and now yourself. And it is quickly and strangely you have come. I did not see you walking up this hillside, that most men fear to tread upon."

Still the stranger smiled. "I go through this land to my own. Perhaps you did not see me coming, Lord, because you were so busy with your work. What are you doing?"

"I am hanging a thief that I caught robbing me." For one second Manawyddan's sea-gray eyes met his and flashed like sunlit ice.

"Then where is the thief, Lord? I see only ourselves, and something moving in that glove you have laid out there: something that can be no bigger than a mouse. It ill becomes a man of such birth and breeding as yours to handle vermin like that, Lord. Let it go free."

His tone cajoled, but his eyes clung to Manawyddan's, that he thought he had caught at last. They pulled and drew, as softly and inexorably as the tide pulls the swimmer caught in its silken-soft, irresistible might.

With a tearing effort Manawyddan pulled his eyes away. "I will not, by the Mothers! Stealing from me I found it, and it shall die."

The stranger took a little bag out from under his cloak. From that he took silver, which he tossed up and down so that it sparkled in the sun. It sparkled too much. Manawyddan strove to look away from it and could not; knew that he had been trapped.

"Lord, this is all the little store I got in Lloegyr, by singing and by begging. I will give it all to you if you will let that vermin go."

Again, with an effort that it seemed might tear his eyes from their sockets, Manawyddan pulled his eyes away. "By the Mothers! I will neither free it nor sell it."

"As you will." The singer put his silver away, shrugged, and walked off down the other side of the Mound.

Manawyddan bent to place the cross-stick on the two forks of the gallows, but his hands were shaking so that for a little while he could not do it. He was getting it fixed in place at last when he stopped, his hands frozen in midair.

A druid was coming now, by his white dress and gold ornaments one high among the followers of Keridwen, the Dark Queen of the Lake, the Goddess that is older than any God. As indeed is only fitting, since She-That-Brings-Forth is the first symbol of creation known to man.

"Good day to you, Lord." His deep voice had the tone of a harp.

Manawyddan showed him proper respect. This time he asked no questions, but it was not long before he found himself answering them. With surprise he heard himself saying more than he meant to say, though his eyes were safely fixed on the ground. "The creature is in the shape of a mouse, Lord, but I caught it robbing me."

Again the shocked protest, again the offer to buy. This time gold was offered, and Manawyddan had to raise his eyes, he could find no excuse to keep them lowered. The druid held the gold pieces in his right hand, above his cupped left. Up and down he tossed them, up and down. They shone like falling stars. They were growing bigger. They were too bright for moons. They glowed like blazing, falling suns . . .

He heard his own voice saying harshly, "I will neither sell it nor set it free." The voice seemed to come from another man's throat, from a self deeper than the self he knew. "As it ought, so shall it die."

"Well, do as you please, Lord." The druid, too, shrugged and went away.

Manawyddan sank to his knees beside the tiny gallows. His whole body trembling, he covered his face with his hands. Would he have strength for another battle?

When he thought that his hand was steady enough, he made a tiny noose, then quickly opened the glove. His fingers shot in and grasped his prey.

She screamed once, a pitiful little scream such as a mouse might give in the teeth of a cat, then thrashed from side to side, kicking, biting so fiercely that he could hardly hold her. Somehow he got the noose about her neck.

She went limp then, like a woman fainting, and for the first time he saw her body clearly. Saw and understood why she had been less quick and light in her flight than the others. He flinched and turned away his head, for the son of Llyr was a kindly man. Nevertheless he swung her tiny, furry body toward the gallows.

Then stopped, as he had stopped before, his victim almost falling from his nerveless hand.

Up the side of the Mound a High Druid was coming, riding in a golden chariot, and in his hand a sickle shining golden in the sun. Tall he was, and white-robed, and brighter than the gold glowed the crystal ring on the hand that held the sickle. That ring was of the holy mystic stone called *Glain Neidr;* that stone is made by serpents, and both its making and its using are among the Mysteries.

Behind him his following stretched down to the plain; splendidly dressed men in splendid chariots of bronze, drawn by the finest horses that the son of Llyr had ever seen. How far that line stretched he could not tell, yet he knew that it was better to look at it than into the face of the High Druid, and one quick flashing glance at those oncoming men told him much.

Their eyes were too bright, as their Lord's own were too bright, yet each man's eyes were subtly, strangely vacant. Not of sight, but of self. Each was like a single facet of a jewel, mirroring but a single beam of the light that blazed through those tremendous, sunlike, Otherworldly eyes that shone through the whole company as through a mask.

Eyes that must blaze directly from the High Druid's own proud, serene face.

Manawyddan clutched the mouse closer. With his free hand he set the point of his knife at its throat.

"Your blessing, Lord Druid." Reverently he spoke, looking carefully past that noble, high-held head.

"You have it, my son." The deep voice seemed to enfold him like water, with the depth and softness and strength of sun-warmed water. To lap at the edges of his mind steadily, gently, inexorably, as waves lap at the rocks that in the end they will wear away.

"Is not that a mouse in your hand, my son?"

Still that soft, enfolding pressure, tightening a little, like a snake's coils . . .

Courage came to Manawyddan. He raised his eyes and met those eyes that were beaming mildly, benevolently, too dazzlingly, upon him. Eyes that he knew, yet now was seeing more fully than he ever had seen them before, their unearthliness burning through the veils.

"It is a mouse," he said, "and she has robbed me."

Still those dazzling eyes beamed mildly, benevolently upon him. "Well, since I have come in the hour of this vermin's doom, I will ransom it from you. We who are Lords of Life like not to see the taking of life. Especially when the creature is with young, and so sacred to the Mothers."

"By the Mothers themselves, I will not free it!"

"Look first at the ransom I offer."

But this time Manawyddan turned his eyes away from the shower of gold, and would not look. Not though its luster seemed to fill the air around the High Druid as though with fire. Not though it glowed so fiercely that the sun-brightness of it burned through his closed eyelids.

"I will give you all this gold and more than the gold." Again the deep voice enfolded him. "I will give you all these horses you see here and upon the plain, and I will give you the chariots they draw, and all the treasures they carry."

"I will not set the beast free." Somehow Manawyddan got the words out. It was hard, hard as pushing heavy stones uphill, yet he knew that he was winning. The unearthly force that was in him, as in all men, was standing firm. Eyes and voice were losing their power over him slowly, bit by bit.

But now the resonant deep voice changed; grew stern. "You who come of the Kings of the Old Tribes will violate the Ancient Harmonies? Slay the mother who is heavy with young?"

The hand that held the sickle was lifted, as if to curse. But it was no fear of curse or sickle that made Manawyddan shrink back, made his tortured hands close tighter on knife and mouse. The light of the ring, of the *Glain Neidr,* was burning through his closed lids. Burning with terrible, unguessable splendor, burning him with all the cold fire in all the eyes of all the snakes that ever lived . . .

He could see it. He could see that shining death as clearly as if his eyes were open and he held it in his own hand.

Desperately, agonizingly, he raised up other images to set between himself and it. The face of Rhiannon, young and tender, as a ray of moonlight fell upon it that night when he begot Pryderi. That same face, aged but more deeply beautiful, that second night when she lay beside him at Arberth, knowing him now, truly his. Pryderi himself, laughing and playing with his dogs; the dogs that the Mound had swallowed.

He opened his eyes; he looked straight into the eyes of his tormentor. Not striving to match sparkling fire with fire, but with that sea-cold, sea-gray look that had been Llyr's. That kept always its own chill, quiet depths.

"I will take no price that you have offered, O Gray Man, Son of Him that Hides in the Wood.

That, I think, is near enough to one of your names, and another, I am sure, is Death."

That sparkling, beaming radiance ceased to beam and sparkle. Clouds boiled up suddenly, blotting out the sun. All that long train of chariots, men, and beasts shook, wavered, and winked out. Only the bare gray hillside was left. Gray too was that Lord who sat there in his golden chariot, alone but not diminished, baleful yet defeated, for all his measureless might.

"Name your own price, man of earth. I will pay it."

"Set Rhiannon and Pryderi free."

For a breath's space the iron jaw tightened, the deep eyes that until that day Manawyddan had met only in dreams shone with all the serpent fires that had blazed in the ring.

"You shall have them. Set the mouse free."

"I will have more. Take the enchantment and glamour off Dyved. Put back the people and beasts and houses as they were before."

"That will take longer. To gather together souls that have been born and reborn into butterfly after butterfly, dragonfly after dragonfly—that is not the work of a moment."

"Yet you will do it."

"I will."

Mists covered the earth below. The Mound became an island in a gray sea of fog. Presently the Gray Man said; "The charm is working. Set her free."

"Not yet," said Manawyddan.

In his hand the mouse struggled and cried pitifully; she had wakened from her swoon. Her small bright eyes strained longingly toward the Gray Man. So a woman in mortal fear cries out to the man she loves.

"I will not let her go until I know what all this is about," said Manawyddan.

"Hear then. I am a King in my own world, as once I was a King here on earth. And Gwawl the Bright is my friend—the man whom her father chose for Rhiannon. He still lies in his bed, sick with the bruises of Pwyll's beating. For in our world that wrong was done less than three nights ago, though in yours, where time rushes by like a frightened horse, trampling all, Pwyll has grown old and died."

"Pwyll sought only to get back what was his own. The woman had a right to choose her man."

"And she chose like a fool. She who might still be Gwawl's new-married bride, young and lovely— what is she now? You know best, who have kissed her wrinkles and tasted her temper. All the worlds I know of—and I know of many—are but training grounds, schoolrooms for those to follow. But how a woman so mulishly self-willed as Rhiannon ever reached the Bright World I do not know. She belonged on earth, and she returned to earth."

"Then you should have left her there." Manawyddan's own jaw tightened. "You yourself— have you grown so far above us? You, who to avenge a few weals on the back of a man who tried to take a woman against her will, had a babe torn from its mother's arms to be the prey of a monster of the Underworld."

The Gray Man smiled faintly, wearily. "When I did that I had just seen Gwawl's back, and those few weals you speak of were fresh and not so few. Never will I forget that outrage; it is beyond your understanding, man of a low, gross world. In Annwn, the first world above yours, there is still violence; Pwyll won Arawn's friendship by killing for him.* But in the Bright World we have outgrown violence. We still war, but with magic and trickery, we who have far more brain than you to trick with—and other powers you cannot dream of. We hate the sight and smell of blood, and any sight or sound of the pain of the body. Those gross evils we have banished."

"I am glad to hear it," said Manawyddan dryly, "considering how long you have held Rhiannon and Pryderi prisoners."

"I have not hurt them," said the Gray Man. "Though I have taken pains to inconvenience them, and wish now that I had taken more." He sighed. "Rhiannon did evil—such evil as the Bright World had never seen—when she plotted that violence against Gwawl. For that blasphemous invasion I blasted all Dyved; I meant to keep it a desert forever."

"So you might have had you let well enough alone. Had you been satisfied with the capture of Rhiannon and Pryderi I never could have reached you."

The Gray Man said grimly; "You sowed grain where I would have no grain grow. You made fruitful a tiny patch of My wilderness."

"A small patch, surely. Kigva and I were not young lovers who might have repeopled the land."

*See the First Branch of the *Mabinogi*.

"You did enough. You set yourself against My will. Twice the men of my household and my foster-brothers came to punish you; as bulls and as stags they trampled your fields. But on the third night my wife and the ladies of my court wanted a share of the sport, so I turned them into mice. You think you have outwitted me, mortal fool, but had she not been with child, you never could have overtaken her. Now let her go."

"Not yet," said Manawyddan. "Swear me an oath that never again shall any enchantment be put on Dyved."

"I swear it. Let her go."

In the gray twilight that he had made, the Gray Man was changing. Strange lights and colors were playing over his face and body, that seemed to shift and unshape and reshape beneath them, not being fast in one form like the bodies that we know. Again Manawyddan felt danger.

"You will take one more oath," he said. "To take no more vengeance on Pryderi or Rhiannon, and none on me, forever."

For a breath's space the Gray Man's shifting shape became black as night. It shot up and towered above Manawyddan, reaching almost to the clouds. From his eyes flashed such lightnings that it seemed the old terrible thunder must break again over the Mound. Then he shrank back again to the size of a tall man. He beamed again, mildly, amused, with genuine respect.

"I swear that. And by the Mothers. It was good thinking in you to ask it. Otherwise the whole trouble would have come upon you."

"For fear of that I chose my words with care," said Manawyddan.

"Now give me my wife," said the Gray Man.

"Not until I see mine free before me. And our son with her."

"Look! There they are coming," said the Gray Man.

From the east came a sudden barking of dogs, the sudden sound of laughter. Manawyddan started and whirled around, for he knew that laughter. Pryderi was running toward him, his hair streaming red-gold on the wind, his dogs leaping joyously about him, while he laughed as joyously.

Neither man knew what made him turn his head . . .

From the west Rhiannon was coming, and in her face was a deep gladness, a new wisdom. The gladness outshone the gold of her robe, that was such a dress of shimmering light as she had worn when first she appeared to Pwyll upon that same Mound, long ago; only shot with silver now, as her hair was shot with silver. But never had she looked more beautiful to any man than she looked to Manawyddan now.

He set the mouse down, gently. He ran to meet those two, and they ran to meet him. The *Mabinogi* does not tell us whose arms first closed upon whom, but for a little while all three must have clung together, close as one body. What they said is not told either, and perhaps it is right that it is not, for those words and that hour belonged to them only, and perhaps the words would not have made sense to anybody else, anyway.

When at last they turned, the Gray Man had

become a shape of gray cloud. Only his eyes were still human, if indeed they had ever been human. Beside him in the chariot sat a young woman lovely as morning. Even her shape was wonder and invitation and delight; it may be that in the higher worlds, approaching motherhood is not disfiguring as it is here.

Manawyddan walked across to them. He faced that grayness that was still a Mystery and a mighty Power.

"Do not think that I am gloating over my own cleverness, Lord. Well I know that of us two you are by far the mightier. But throughout our struggle I loved and you hated; ask yourself what difference that made. Ask yourself too—you who think I cannot understand what you felt when you saw your friend's back—what you would have felt had you seen your brother writhing in the agony of a poisoned wound. Had you had to cut his head off with your own hand to end his pain."

The Grayness darkened a little, as sometimes a storm cloud darkens. The eyes did not change.

"Indeed, I did underestimate you, mortal. You played your game well. Lamenting in the fields and grumbling in the house, and letting the anger over your loss flow free over the surface of your mind, while you kept the depths clean and cool— all so that I would think you a common man, a mere murderous earth-fool who might slay my Queen."

"So you could see into my mind," said Manawyddan. "I was not sure."

For a moment the Grayness turned back into a man again. It smiled. "We can always see into your minds, earth-fool. We can see your thoughts and if we please we can play with them, as a cat with mice. Use you as the tiny beings of the air use you, they that you cannot see, yet that bring sickness and death on you. Wise men of the future will learn that much—soon, as I count time—but in their puffed-up pride it will never occur to them that they are being used by their betters as well as by their inferiors."

"If you mean that we are only your puppets," said Manawyddan, "I do not believe you. We can think of enough ways to hurt ourselves."

"I do not deny it. And of yourselves, as you have said, you can love. Most of the time we leave you to your own folly—but sometimes we have a purpose that you can serve."

"Not often, I hope," said Manawyddan.

"No. And when we do, we usually help you, as the higher should help the lower. I think that no Lord of the Bright World will invade earth openly again. Mind is growing stronger, even among mortal men, and the walls between the worlds are growing firmer. We may play with your thoughts again, but only with your thoughts."

"Remember your oath, and do not play with mine, Lord. I have had enough of playing cat to your mouse."

Those last words reminded Manawyddan of something. He turned to that young Queen of the Bright World. "I am sorry to have put fear and trouble on you, Lady, but I was sorely pressed."

She smiled. "Truly you put fear on me, Lord. Had you hanged me, my child would have had to find another body, and my Lord might have had to search long for my soul. It might have fallen into Arawn's hands, and have been kept from Him long and long."

"Speaking of souls," said the Gray Man, "my task is done. Look down upon your land."

As he spoke, the clouds rolled away from the sun, and the mists vanished from the land below.

And Manawyddan looked, and saw the fields of Dyved all golden with grain. He saw herds and houses, as of old. He saw the smoke rising from the housewives' cooking fires, and he heard faintly the songs of the reapers.

"It is good," Rhiannon breathed beside him. "It is good." Her hand slipped into his.

On his other side Pryderi squeezed his arm and pranced. "It is glad Kigva will be to see us, especially me!"

They three were alone upon the Mound. Chariot and Grayness and that Queen from the Bright World—none of them were anywhere. Like dreams from which a sleeper wakens, they had gone.

15

The Seven Years End

At twilight the son of Llyr sat outside the Palace of Arberth. Its seven years' silence was over; it hummed like a beehive, and through those many noises, all of which sounded good now, he could hear the three he most wanted to hear: Rhiannon's, light and brisk, talking with her maids as they cooked supper; Pryderi's and Kigva's, laughing and teasing each other. He thought of what Rhiannon had told him, her mouth curving in that tender, half-wicked smile whose wisdom was not quite of earth.

"Tonight I think they will get that son they have longed for."

And her hand had touched his, and her eyes had made promises; they too would have joy that night, though their child-getting days were over.

He thought it would be pleasant to see his grandchild grow and play about Arberth, as he had not been there to see Pryderi play; a smallness and a round pink chubbiness, some tears and many yells, and a great deal of laughter . . .

The bogey came out of the bushes and looked at him. "Good evening to you, Lord," he said, "and goodbye."

"Why go? You have been a good friend."

"I know I have," said the bogey. "I am not embarrassed because I did not go up onto the Mound with you; I could have done nothing there. I did catch the mouse."

"You did indeed."

"And for that you never could thank me enough. But I can do no more for you. Rhiannon does not need me, and besides, she can see me, and that would make it risky to play tricks on her. I did manage to play a few on Kigva, in spite of you."

"Are you sure of that?"

"Yes." The bogey grinned. "I can afford to own up now. I am going back to the shepherd's hut. They need me there. I can do things for them and to them, and make them marvel at my cleverness."

"Do not do too many things to them . . . And good luck be with you."

"And with you, Lord." The bogey vanished.

Manawyddan sat alone again, and wondered if he had ever really played any tricks on Kigva, or had only boasted of what he would have liked to do.

He rose and walked a little way from the palace and listened to the hum of the evening. To the gentle music of the open fields, it that at nightfall is more soothing than any other sound of earth. He saw those fields, their gold dulled by the twilight, and above them the white width of the sky, vast beyond belief; darkening now, yet pure still with the purity of its unearthliness that mirrored the infinite. He heard the low chirping of birds, settling themselves for sleep, and he smiled. Good to be alive—alive, and with work to do, and those you loved around you. What better lot could there be in any world?

But in the Bright World, on his fabulous throne made of the stuff of sunsets, shining red-gold with their heavenly fires, the Gray Man may have sat and smiled. *You have worked hard and fought hard, son of Llyr, and for a few days of My time you have won. But your son has not faced his last foe.*

And in Gwynedd, in the Court of Don, the child called Gwydion, heir of Gwynedd, he whose greatness Taliesin had foretold, sat and played with his toys. As one day he, a man, would sit alone in the strange, rich chambers of his own brain and devise ways to play with other playthings. With men themselves, like fate . . .

THE FATE OF THE CHILDREN OF LLYR, AND THE END OF THE THIRD BRANCH.

For Pedants and Some Others

My original rule was never to alter anything I found in The Four Branches of the Mabinogi, whatever I might add or subtract. But if I have not broken this rule in my treatment of the Third Branch, I have at least bent it considerably.

I have changed the disappearing magic "castle" into a disappearing magic opening in the side of the Mound of Arberth. But since castles came into Britain with the Norman Conquest, I assume that this one was a monkish addition. Chambered tombs, buried inside great mounds, are a definite part of the Celtic picture, though probably they were built by pre-Celtic peoples.

Since the location of Arberth seems to be debatable—the late Professor W.J. Grufydd said that the traditional site would not be appropriate for the capital of Dyved—I have taken the liberty of placing it near the Preseli Mountains, where we are definitely told that his nobles conferred with Pwyll—or, rather, gave him orders.

Geologists agree that the Preseli Mountains must have been the original home of Stonehenge's famous "bluestones," so that gave me another batch of ideas. It also provided motivation for Pryderi's somewhat mysterious mounting of the

Mound. The *Mabinogion* does not consider it necessary to say why he suddenly took it into his head to do such a risky thing, but we modern authors have to give our characters reasons for their most unreasonable actions. We lack the glorious freedom of the old bards, and perhaps that is just as well.

I take it that the original Mound, wherever it stood (or did not stand), had attached to it some grim pagan ritual which the monkish transcribers of the *Mabinogion* either did not understand or wished to suppress.

They also probably did not think that magic powers should be attributed to so good a man as Manawyddan, but he belonged to the mightiest kingly house in the Four Branches, and of these royal houses Sir John Rhys said: ". . . the kings are mostly the greatest magicians of their time . . . the ruling class in these stories . . . had their magic handed down from generation to generation." So I have felt free to de-whitewash Manawyddan and have him perform several of the magic tricks attributed to his Irish counterpart, Manannan mac Lir. The resemblance of one of these to the famous Hindu "rope trick" seems to me very interesting.

If Gawain's renowned "Green Knight" really should be called the Gray Knight, as many think, (Irish *glas* meaning either gray or green), a connection with our Gray Man seems clear. And in his fascinating *The Corpse and the King,* the distinguished scholar Heinrich Zimmer identified this mysterious Knight with Death Himself.

The amazing saga of a world that evolution has cursed